THE HIGH SEAS OF MARS

RED FRONTIER BOOK 4

GAYNE C. YOUNG

SIX CONTINENTS COMMUNICATIONS

1

———————

Powell's helmet caved inward at the impact.

Shards of high-molecular-weight polyethylene splintered from the protective cover and drove into his scalp just above his left ear. He fell backwards. His finger jerked the trigger of his HK Urban Assault Viper rifle, unleashing a torrent of automatic fire. Bullets strafed the alley. Spent shell casings plinked over the broken concrete ground. Powell fell into Taylor and the two men collapsed in a heap upon the ground.

"Off!" Taylor screamed.

He rolled the semi-conscience Powell off his chest and looked up to see a giant perched over him. The gargantuan's skin was light mahogany in color and so whelped as to resemble that of a reptile. The abomination bellowed forth in rage, raised the heavy metal pipe in his hands well over his head, then brought it down towards Taylor's head. Taylor rolled to his left. The pipe struck the ground with a deafening thud. Taylor raised the rifle slung at his chest and fired twice. The giant's right thigh blew outward in a spray of blood and muscle. The goliath howled in immediate response. He grabbed the rifle before him by the barrel, wretched in from Taylor's hands, and tossed it aside. Taylor reached for the pistol at his upper leg.

The giant grabbed Taylor, hoisted him above his head, and brought him down on his left knee. Taylor's heard his spine crack and felt several disks slip. The wind was forced from his lungs. He gasped in pain and in the panic of needing air. The giant dropped Taylor to the ground. Taylor splayed outward. He reached once more for his pistol. The giant lunged downward, grabbed Taylor, and swung him sideways and into a wall. Taylor groaned in pain at the impact. The giant ripped Taylor's plate carrier vest from his body. Taylor jerked his pistol free from his holster. The giant thrust forward and took Taylor's gun hand in his and squeezed. Taylor howled in sheer pain. He felt the small bones in his hand grinding against one another. The giant grabbed Taylor by the neck with his other hand and lifted him off the ground and to before him. Taylor fought for air. The giant tightened his grip on Taylor's gun hand and neck. Taylor's vision went blurry.

His head spun.

Two quick shots rang out.

The side of the giant's head blew outwards. The gargantuan teetered sideways then collapsed. Taylor kicked himself free from the fallen hulk and spun around to see Powell leaning against the wall, a rifle at his shoulder.

"Thanks," Taylor gasped.

Powell nodded and walked towards the fallen body. He lowered his rifle and put two shots in anger into the fallen giant's head.

"God damn Descendants!" Powell spat on what was left of the giant's face. "Inbred pieces a' shit the whole lot of them."

Taylor pulled his vest back over his chest, holstered his pistol, and collected his rifle.

"You saved me," Taylor coughed.

"You were getting your ass kicked for sure," Powell laughed. "I almost held off to see if your eyes were going to pop out of your skull. They sure looked like they were going to."

Taylor shook his head and smirked.

"Asshole."

The men's joking and recovery was interrupted by a sudden

cacophony of gunfire. The alley wall behind Taylor and Powell sparked with the impact of bullets and ricochets. The men spun around and dropped into a kneeling position with their rifles before them.

"Looks like the whole favela," Powell said of the massive crowd rushing down the twisted and broken alley toward them.

Taylor estimated the mob being more than 60 in number. It consisted of men, women, and children. All were Descendants and all were armed with some kind of weapon. Some carried rifles and pistols and others carried metal pipes, rocks, chains, and weaponry fashioned from found items or those collected along the alley.

"Holy shit," Taylor declared under his breath.

The walls behind Taylor and Powell continued sparking with the impact of errant bullets. Screams of anger and rage echoed down the alley.

"Call it!" Powell barked. He pumped a 20 mm shell into the grenade launcher below the barrel of his rifle and fired into the oncoming onslaught. The grenade rocketed forward 25 yards and exploded in front of the crowd unleashing dozens of lonsdaleite blades. The harder than diamond shards ripped through flesh and bone with ease. The mass spread out and those who were still standing tended to those on the ground who were writhing in pain or in the shock of missing a limb or half a face.

"Headquarters, this is 1836," Taylor barked into the radio affixed to his vest at his left shoulder. "I've got 60 hostiles approaching down alley north of our position."

The mob rushed forward. They discarded the wounded, collected the fallen's weapons, and stormed down the alley and towards the two soldiers. Powell stood and pulled Taylor up by the shoulder. The two backed slowly down the alley keeping their rifles at the ready and aimed at the oncoming mob of Descendants.

"You're looking at the tip of the iceberg," a voice crackled over the radio. "You got two groups just as large coming down from the east four blocks out."

"Shit!" Powell hissed through gritted teeth. He thought for a moment then asked, "Miller's group?"

"Down," the voice on the radio answered in a solemn tone. "Nothing between you and them. Phillips and Corman to the west are pulling out."

"Dammit," Taylor huffed.

Powell cursed under his breath then commanded into his radio, "Light it up."

"Affirmative," the radio cackled. "Five minutes out."

The two soldiers turned down a narrow alley and headed west. The favela was built upon uneven ground and fabricated of concrete, tin, tarpaper, cardboard, and salvaged auto parts. The backstreet they ran through was dark and slicked in runoff from open sewers and rotting garbage. It was an obstacle course of discarded items, broken machinery, and household garbage. They ran down and around this and under electric cables running between buildings haphazardly, strings of drying laundry, and open windows.

They turned a corner and immediately came upon a group of three men standing with their weapons at their sides. The group caught sight of the two soldiers and yelled warnings to one another as they raised their rifles. Taylor and Powell fired on the go and the three men were knocked backwards at the shots and to the ground. Taylor and Powell continued running forward. They jumped over the fallen men and continued down the winding narrow alley. A gaunt woman as white as snow and covered in tattoos burst from an open doorway just before them. She aimed her pistol before her and fired three times in quick succession. The second bullet caught Powell just above his right knee and he stumbled forward and rolled to the ground. Taylor put two rifle shots into the woman's chest, and she spun around 180° and collapsed in a twisted heap.

"A pipe to the head and then some idiot bitch shoots me damn near in the knee," Powell grunted. "This just ain't my day."

Taylor knelt and quickly examined his friend's injury.

"In and out," Taylor declared. "Missed everything important."

Powell hastily pulled a small paper packet from a pocket on his vest, tore it open, and poured the powdered contents in and around his wound.

Taylor grabbed his friend under his arms to help him stand, then was knocked to the ground by an unseen charge.

The man stood just under six feet tall. His face was palsied and heavily tattooed. He and Taylor rolled over and off of Powell and to the ground. The man reared back with knife in hand and brought it down at Taylor's throat. Taylor caught the Descendant's wrist, stopping the blade mere centimeters from entering his neck. A single gunshot rang out and the man's face vaporized into a heavy red mist. Taylor pushed the faceless man off of him and scrambled to his feet.

"That's two ya' owe me," Powell exclaimed.

Heavy gunfire erupted.

Taylor stumbled back at the sudden impact at his chest. He looked down to see Powell's right shoulder explode outward in a heavy rain of fabric, blood, and muscle.

Powell grunted in pain then pumped another shell into his grenade launcher and fired into the mob rushing towards him and Taylor. The grenade rocketed forward and exploded into the crowd some 25 yards up the alley. Bodies vaulted upward at the explosion. Flesh and blood rained downward and painted the narrow alley walls.

And yet the mob continued forward.

They drove over and through one another and down the alley like some berserker poured from one heavily driven mindset. The mass fired on the run. Powell caught a bullet to his left thigh. Then one in the center of his protective vest. His body spasmed and jerked at the impact. He unleashed a torrent of gunfire into the approaching mob, and yelled over his shoulder, "Go!"

Taylor ignored the command. He fired into the massive juggernaut then rushed to his downed friend but shot backward at two heavy impacts to his vest. He caught his footing and rushed once more towards Powell.

"Go!" Powell ordered without turning around. "Go now!"

A faint whistle called across the sky above the favelas. Taylor looked up then back to his watch.

"Go!" Powell screamed above the melee of violence in the alley.

Taylor hesitated then turned. Something stung his neck and he grabbed it as if trying to catch the pain. He pulled his hand back to see his palm smeared in blood. A heavy blow crashed into his back. He stumbled forward then used the momentum to start running. He ran down the alley ignoring the sounds of gunfire, the ricocheting of bullets against the walls and street around him, and the horde's screams of unrelenting rage.

The whistle's twisted howl grew sharper. Taylor heard the impact far behind him then launched forward and through the air as the percussion blast thundered down the alley. A wave of heat crashed over him. The air vanished. Everything before him was painted in the red shadows of flames. He rocketed down the alley then slammed to the ground and somersaulted uncontrollably down an incline and succumbed to darkness.

2

"Ah, it's a baby," Link joked in a child-like voice.

"Hardly worth dragging aboard," Alex complained on an exhale of cigarette smoke.

Hall ignored the comments and instead studied the beast writhing on deck. Hall put the great white shark at just under 11 feet in length and carrying a weight of about 500 pounds. True, it was half the size of the sharks he and the crew normally hauled from the sea, but it would make them money all the same.

Hall had seen thousands of white sharks of the size before him in his 20 years aboard the *Aurora* and all had brought in enough money to make the killing and butchering of them worth the time and effort.

"Anything over 10 feet's worth more than our time," Hall declared to the group.

The crew nodded in understanding and Donnie stepped forward.

"Hold 'em tight," Donnie instructed.

Link and Alex tightened their grips on their long-handled gaffs embedded in either side of the shark's body.

"Even the smaller ones got fight in 'em every now and again," Donnie jokingly continued.

He walked towards the shark. The cadaverous gray monster

thrashed. Link and Alex held tight on their gaffs. Donnie continued forward. He positioned himself next to and above the shark's head, placed his bolt pistol at the center point between the beast's eyes, and fired. A small dagger shaped bolt rocketed into the great white's brain, expanded outward, then retracted back up and into the pistol. The shark spasmed violently and shook then lay still.

"Come on," Hall commanded. "Back to work."

The great white was dragged a short distance and dropped into the hold where two butchers awaited. They would quickly gut the shark, piece it out, then pack it on ice. Almost every part of the fish would be utilized. The organs and meat would be sold as food, the hide as leather, the cartilage skeleton and fins and select organs for traditional medicines, and its jaws sold as curios.

Donnie holstered his bolt pistol and returned to the command console at the stern of the boat. He reengaged the electric winch and watched as yard after yard of thin cable was pulled in from the sea.

The 107-foot-long *Aurora* ran 40 miles of line with baited hooks set every 20 feet. The ship targeted great whites but occasionally hooked hammerhead, tiger, and mako sharks. Although these were harvested, they were considered a secondary species and fetched far less money at market. The *Aurora's* lines also hooked sea turtles, squid, and the occasional bird. It was the latter that drew Hall's attention away from his peering down into the hold.

"Damn bird," Hall said, looking out past the stern to an enormous albatross struggling high above the ocean. The bird had a wingspan of over 14 feet and was a ghostly white.

Hall left the edge of the hold and made his way to a locker just below the wheelhouse. He removed a 12-gauge pump shotgun and walked to the stern of the craft.

"You want me to cut the line?" Donnie asked of the line the bird was attached to. "Looks like some ugly ass kite, don't it, the way it's flying around attached to that line."

Hall ignored the question and the comments that followed. He pumped a round into the shotgun, drew aim on the bird, and fired.

The albatross shattered into a cloud of feathers. Flesh and blood rained down upon the sea.

"Bad luck shooting an albatross," Donnie exclaimed. "You should know that as long as you've been at sea."

Hall placed the shotgun in a stand next to the winch controls.

"I've been at sea long enough to know that that's bullshit," Hall laughed.

The winch suddenly stopped.

The boat went dead. Its diesel engines quieted.

Donnie frantically worked the winch controls.

"What the hell?!" Donnie angrily questioned.

Hall watched Donnie's attempt to reengage the winch then spun around at Captain Lun calling down from the wheelhouse.

"You lock that up again?" Captain Lun questioned.

"No," Hall answered as he walked toward the wheelhouse. "Everything just went dead."

The captain walked down the narrow stairway and towards the deck. He paused halfway down to stare at something off the starboard side.

Hall saw this and turned in the same direction. He didn't see anything out of the ordinary at first but then slowly saw what he believed to be a mirage. It was a shimmer of light, a distortion of some kind. He had never seen anything like it in all his years at sea.

The air was cut by a sudden crack followed by a sharp whistle.

Something struck the side of the wheelhouse with a heavy thud.

The object clanged to the deck.

Hall's eyes locked on the object. He started to yell in warning to the others but was too slow.

The stun grenade exploded unleashing a blinding flash of light and a deafening crack of thunder. Hall and those behind him were thrown to the deck by the blast. Captain Lun stumbled backwards, rolled down the staircase, and onto the deck.

Hall immediately fought to stand.

He felt dizzy.

His head throbbed in agonizing pain.

The world around him spun.

He felt he might vomit.

His hearing slowly returned.

His vision slowly recovered.

He heard a crashing thud above him. He gazed upward to see another grenade dropping toward him. The grenade landed at his feet. He lunged for the small canister, took it in his hand, and tossed it before him and overboard. The grenade detonated in an explosion of seawater that shot forth a geyser some 30 feet upward. A shimmer ran through the deck of the boat.

Hall looked about to ensure the rest of the crew was okay. He locked eyes with Donnie. The man nodded for some reason and Hall nodded in return unsure of why he was doing such.

Hall stood then took a moment to steady himself. He was still dizzy but found the sensation slowly subsiding. He looked out and across to see that the unexplainable shimmer was gone. In its place set an enormous black ship some three times larger than that of the *Aurora*. It was a military ship of some sort and armed to the teeth with weaponry. A smaller craft raced from the battleship. This boat also resembled some craft of military design and had more than a dozen men of various ethnicities, sizes, and shapes. All were weathered and aged by the elements, heavily armed, and carried looks of anger and rage. The craft sped forward cutting the deep blue water with hurried ease.

"Prepared to be..."

Hall's warning was interrupted by a hail of gunfire. Bullets screamed through the air, stitched across into the side of the ship, upon the deck, and into the wheelhouse.

Hall dove for cover. The gunfire continued.

The approaching boat's engine roared.

Hall covered his head in protection from the falling shrapnel. Errant chucks of lead fell upon the outside of his hands, neck, back, and legs. He screamed in fright and the fear that the storm of violence would never end.

The gunfire suddenly ceased.

The approaching craft's engine diminished.

Metal clanged against the sides of the ship.

Hall uncovered his head and looked upward to see a grappling hook catch on the guardrail. A pair of boots dropped onto the deck next to Hall. They were followed by another pair and then another.

"Up!" a voice boomed across the deck.

Hall stood.

The others in his crew followed.

There were 10 men, all dressed in mismatched body armor of varying camo patterns, all sunburned and weathered, and all holding a rifle, pistol, or machete or combination of all three. The clear leader of this group stood just under six feet tall. He was thin yet muscled and his face was pockmarked and scarred. His eyes were coal black. He wore a bulletproof vest covered in black and gray digital camo and had across this a bandolier of grenades. He wore a pistol in a holster at his right thigh and held before him a rifle designed for close combat.

Captain Lun stepped before the presumed pirate leader.

"What is this?" the captain nervously asked. "We are under the protection of Kantar Saber."

The pirate leader let his slinged rifle drop to his side. He pulled his pistol and jammed the barrel into the captain's eye socket.

"Kantar Saber no longer controls the Great Northern Sea."

Captain Lun shook in fear. He fought to swallow.

The pirate leader smirked and pulled the trigger. The pistol belched forward a .45 slug that nearly halved the captain's skull. Blood, skull fragments, and brain tissue exploded outward, and the near headless body collapsed. The crew of the *Aurora* trembled in shock at the execution and of the actions they feared would follow.

The pirate leader stepped over the captain's fallen body and toward the crowded bunch of crew members. He raised his pistol to Hall's forehead.

"Name?" the pirate demanded.

Hall fought to speak.

His mouth was bone dry, and his jaw seemed locked. He fought this and finally spoke.

"Hall."

The pirate drew his eyes tight, lowered his pistol, and announced, "Hall lives."

Shock washed across Hall's face.

Gunfire erupted across the deck as the pirates unloaded into the remaining crewmen. The men of the *Aurora* danced and spasmed in death as dozens of bullets riddled through their bodies.

The invaders lowered their weapons, The pirate leader walked over the fallen corpses and to the hold. He pulled a grenade from his bandolier and dropped it into the hold. Two screams echoed from the deep interior. The grenade detonated sending forth a column of flame that shot upwards of 20 feet. The *Aurora* shock violently in response and the air took on smell of burning meat and accelerant.

The leader directed two of his men to the winch. The duo approached it and one of them shot the cable attached to it in two with a quick pistol shot. The long cable slunk into the ocean. The two men returned to their kind at the guardrail that they had climbed to get on board.

The leader walked to Hall and commanded his attention.

"Kantar Saber no longer rules the Great Northern Sea."

Hall understood the statement and what his reaction was to be.

"Kantar Saber no longer rules the Great Northern Sea," Hall repeated.

The pirate leader gently slapped Hall's face in fatherly affection, smiled, and returned to his boat.

3

————

The chauffeur opened the rear door of the armored SUV and Shun stepped out of the vehicle and onto the crushed shell road. He took a moment to enjoy the sea air then retrieved a pair of tortoiseshell sunglasses from the pocket of his white linen shirt and put them on.

"Mr. Shun," a man exclaimed as he rushed towards the SUV.

Like Shun, the man was immaculately dressed. He wore cream-colored pants, a pale-yellow long sleeve linen shirt, and espadrilles. His hair was dirty blonde and tousled by the steady breeze off the ocean. "I'm so sorry not to be here to meet you. I saw your vehicle..."

Shun raised his hand to cease the man's explanation.

"It is quite all right," Shun assured the man. "I've only just arrived..."

"And we are very pleased to have you," the man replied, holding out his hand. "I'm Chess. Assistant to Kantar Saber." The two men shook hands. Chess continued, "If you'll follow me."

Shun nodded and followed Chess. The assistant led Shun towards the vast structure that set on piers some 40 feet tall. The two men entered a double wide elevator flanked by two pairs of armed guards at the far end of the structure. The elevator doors closed and the unit rose. A moment later, its wide doors opened to reveal an expansive outdoor room that offered an epic view of the ocean before it. Shun removed his sunglasses to take in the impressive sight.

The room was covered in sisal rugs and the walls were intermittently draped in flowing gauze. A ceiling fan with aluminum blades of which spanned some 40 feet and the breeze off the ocean ensured the area stayed comfortable.

"What have we here?" a joyful voice boomed across the open room.

Shun drew his attention to the blob of a man nearly consumed by an enormous couch at the far end of the room. The man had three armed guards to either side of him while a black and yellow monitor lizard of more than 10 feet slept on the floor before him. The massive reptile wore a leather collar and was chained to a stake to the left of the couch.

Chess stood before Shun and waved his hand in the direction of his boss reclined up on the couch.

"His Excellency, Kantar Saber, Eminence of the Great Northern Sea," Chess announced.

Shun bowed in response.

"It is always a pleasure to see you my friend," Shun said after returning to a standing position.

Kantar smiled and waved to a chair before him.

"Please. Please make yourself comfortable."

Shun nodded and made his way to the chair. He sat then took in the man on the couch before him. Kantar was an enormous individual. He stood roughly 6' 5" tall and easily weighed 450 pounds. He wore a sky-blue sarong, was naked to the waist, was covered in tribal tattoos, and sported long black hair and an almost equally long beard that was adorned with braids and bits of shell. He took a long pull off his hookah hose then exhaled a twisting cloud of smoke.

"Hash," Kantar announced. "A blend of my own creation."

Shun smiled at what served as both an explanation and offer.

"Thank you, but no," Shun said. He pulled a silver cigarette case from his pants pocket and opened it. "But if you will permit me."

"Please," Kantar replied. "Again, make yourself comfortable."

Shun nodded once more then lit his cigarette with a lighter. He placed the instrument back in the cigarette case and placed it on the table to the side of his chair.

A woman of striking beauty with a stunning figure wearing only a sarong and beads of shells around her neck appeared from nowhere. She held before her a wicker tray upon which sat a tall glass of ice and clear liquid. Shun nodded at the half naked woman and took the drink. The

woman bowed then retreated from sight.

Kantar raised an identical glass and toast and declared, "To friends."

"To friends," Shun repeated before taking a sip. The drink was sweet but not overly so and his face showed pleasure at its taste.

Kantar saw this look of elation and explained, "Cane. Also, of my own design."

Shun took a puff on his cigarette.

"As we are friends," Kantar began again, "allow me to get straight to the matter at hand."

Shun took another puff on his cigarette and nodded in agreement.

Kantar drained his drink in one long gulp then returned to his hookah hose. He took in a huge lungful of hash smoke, held it for time, then exhaled.

"Someone is stealing from me!" Kantar suddenly bellowed. "Taking my cargo! Killing my men! Sinking my ships!"

Shun sat unaffected by the sudden outburst. He had known Kantar for decades and was very familiar with his explosive temper. His temper combined with his strength, raw determination, and almost psychotic demeanor were just a few of the traits that had allowed him to advance through the organization so quickly. He had started as a mere soldier in the syndicate but in a matter of just a few years had managed to take the seat as the one who controlled the Great Northern Sea.

Shun pondered this as he sat stoic enjoying his cigarette and the steady breeze coming off the ocean that was ever so stirred by the ceiling fan above him.

Kantar took another huge lungful of hash then ran the fingers of his left hand through his shell-strewn beard.

"This was not the work of locals," Kantar continued. "It is not the work of pirates. These marauders have stealth ships. EMPs..."

Shun tilted his head slightly at the mention of military technology. Advancements such as these were beyond expensive and not readily available on Mars. They were more widely used on what remained of Earth. Whoever was utilizing such technology against Kantar had excellent connections and very deep pockets.

"They destroyed two of my fishing vessels and a Sulphur gas pumping outpost," Kantar continued. His voice was deep and thick with irritation. "They have killed all but one person from each attack."

"Someone to tell the tale," Shun offered.

"Yes," Kantar responded. "And the tales they have told are of flat-out massacre. Of execution. Of the taking of women and children."

Shun took a sip of his drink then lit a fresh cigarette.

"Shun." Kantar paused his smoking to look his friend in the eye. "I need your help."

"Of course," Shun immediately responded. "How may I be of assistance?"

"Whoever is doing this knows my organization far too well. They hit me with almost surgical precision. They know my routes. My crews. My weaknesses."

Shun continued smoking his cigarette, listening intently.

"Given the knowledge these attackers seem to possess, I can only assume—" Kantar paused midsentence. His cheeks were flushed in rage. He took another long drag of hash. "I can only assume that those who are attacking me also work for me!"

The half-naked woman returned with a massive mug of beer in

one hand and a small purse-sized cage in the other. The woman walked to before Kantar who held both hands in want like an unruly child begging for a hug. Kantar took the beer and downed it in a series long, loud gulps. The woman dropped the cage at Kantar's feet then took his empty mug and quickly retreated from sight. Kantar leaned his massive girth forward, reached into the cage, and pulled from it a large rat weighing more than three pounds. The rat writhed in anger and fear in Kantar's massive, clenched fist.

"I want those responsible found!"

Kantar flung the rat in front of the enormous lizard at his feet. The reptile sprung awake, lunged forward, and took the rat in his ink black jaws and swallowed. The lizard arched its neck backward. The lizard shot its tongue outward in a whip-like fashion then collapsed back to the ground and into sleep.

Kantar smiled, leaned back into his couch, and returned to his hookah.

"I want these men found and brought before me. And as these could be my men, because I feel I can trust no one," Kantar continued, "I ask for your help."

Shun took another sip of his drink.

"Find those responsible and bring them to me for punishment."

"It would be my pleasure."

"Of course, I'll pay for your assistance."

Shun drew off the last of his cigarette then placed the butt into the ashtray as his side.

"Friends do not deal in payment," Shun reminded. "Friends deal in favors. And I would be glad to perform one for you."

Kantar smiled at the businessman before him. Unlike him, Shun had rose through the ranks of the organization through business savvy, refined manners, offering favors, and eliminating those not worthy of the aforementioned. Shun was a killer to be sure but the most sophisticated and shrewd of which Kantar had ever encountered

"Thank you," Kantar said. He took another lungful of hash, held it, then exhaled it in a series of large smoke rings.

"I have just the man," Shun offered. "He's an expert in matters such as these."

"An expert dealing with pirates," Kantar chuckled on a cough of smoke.

"An expert with problems," Shun explained. "He's an expert at eliminating them."

4

───────────

"Good morning, Mr. Taylor. Welcome to The Park," Enrique offered from his post behind the welcome desk. "I believe you know the drill."

"I do," Taylor said under his breath.

Enrique watched as the man walked to his desk. Taylor was a large man standing just over 6 foot tall and carrying maybe 210 pounds of muscle. He was barrel chested, wore his dirty blond hair slicked back on top and near shorn on the sides, and had green eyes. His body armor was faded and well-worn, yet he wore it with an air of confidence. Taylor took a semiautomatic pistol from the holster on his leg, a Taser derringer from a holster on his hip, and a straight blade knife from a sideways sheath at the small his back and placed all three weapons in a tray on the table. He then reached for the two pistol magazines affixed to his plate carrier vest.

"That's not necessary, Mr. Taylor," Enrique offered.

Taylor nodded.

An attractive Black woman in her late 40s wearing navy blue scrubs walked down the hall to Taylor.

"You here to see the birthday girl?" she asked of Taylor.

"Jan, good morning," Taylor offered. He stepped forward and to before the nurse. "How is she?"

Jan smiled and placed her hand on Taylor's arm.

"She's doing about the same which as I say is better than getting worse."

Taylor nodded slightly.

"But I know she'll enjoy seeing you."

Taylor nodded again.

"Come on," Jan said as she gently pulled Taylor toward her. She led Taylor down the hall and into a large room bustling with quiet activity. Male and female nurses in bright blue scrubs sat or visited or watched a generally older populace play cards, read, or stare out the window. The ceiling was a hologram of a bright summer sky with gently rolling clouds and matched the world found outside the large windows that encircled the room. A few individuals looked up to watch Taylor and Jan enter the room, but they quickly returned to their private or group activities. Jan led Taylor through and around tables and chairs and overstuffed loveseats and long couches to a window in front of which sat a young woman of 28 years old.

Taylor stopped to look at her. Emily Willis was as beautiful as she had ever been. Her skin was porcelain smooth and in sharp contrast to her long raven black hair. Jan walked to before Emily and knelt and put her hand on Emily's wrist as she spoke. Her voice was soft and warm.

"Emily, Taylor's here. He came to see you for your birthday."

Emily stared at some unseen point outside the window. Jan nodded and stood. She walked to Taylor and ran her hands over his shoulders.

"I'll leave y'all be. I'll be over there if you need anything."

Taylor swallowed and nodded.

"Thank you," he whispered.

Jan left and Taylor went in front of Emily and knelt.

"Emily Dejah Willis," Taylor joyfully exclaimed in the manner in which he had joked with her some 10 years earlier. "How ever are you?"

Emily stared through Taylor and out the window.

Taylor took a moment.

Emily was dressed in a loose-fitting sundress and even in it, Taylor couldn't help but notice her body and the way it filled the dress. Seeing his Dej, as he called her, brought back a swelling of emotions. Being with her sent to the forefront of his conscience growing up with her on the frontier, courting her, their falling in love, then losing her in a series of events brought on by a madman. Taylor did his best to swallow these memories and instead focus on the here and now.

"Jan tells me you're doing well," Taylor said.

He reached out his hand to hold hers then thought the better of it. He instead turned to look out the window. He locked eyes on a birdbath populated by what he recognized as collard sunbirds and lilac breasted rollers. The birds buzzed to and fro in streaks of purple, emerald, and lavender. Taylor wondered if Dej was watching the birds or looking past them to something that only she could see. He wondered what she was staring at and what she was thinking of.

He hoped it was something pleasant.

He hoped that wherever she was she was comfortable and content.

Taylor turned from the birds and back to Dej. He put his hand on hers and if she noticed she showed no reaction. Her hand was soft and warm.

"I asked the chef to make your favorite for your birthday. Homemade chocolate chip ice cream." Taylor gripped her hand tighter. "Is there anything else you'd like?"

Jan walked to in front of Emily's chair. She carried a bouquet of flowers before her.

"Look what just came for you, Emily," Jan almost cooed. "Yellow roses. Aren't they gorgeous?"

Taylor stood and took the card affixed to the arrangement. He returned to his kneeling position before Dej, opened the card, and read.

"To my Dej, happy birthday, yours forever, Taylor."

Dej continued staring out the window.

Taylor ignored this and instead took his love's hand in his once more.

5

———————

The *Ruark* was a dual side ducted fan craft retired from military service and reconfigured as a civilian exploratory ship. It measured just under 17 meters long and 14 meters wide from tip of duct to tip of duct, had a top speed of 150 miles per hour, and was a gift to Taylor from Shun following his exiting the military.

Taylor enjoyed flying the *Ruark*. He found it relaxing and often used the craft as a place to decompress after an assignment. This afternoon was different. This afternoon, piloting the *Ruark* was a chore. He found no relaxation in being at the controls. His mind was still with Dej. He hated what she had become and partially blamed himself for her current state.

He hit the autopilot app on the display screen before him, removed his hands from the controls, and eased back in his seat.

"Enough," Taylor sighed to himself. "Put it behind you."

He closed his eyes and pinched the bridge of his nose. He held that position for a few minutes then opened his eyes and pulled the flask from his vest pocket. He took a long pull of Red Crowe tequila and returned the flask to his vest then checked off the autopilot and took control of the ship. The sky before him was clear free of clouds.

The desert landscape below him was a contrast in color. Rock outcroppings of ivory and beige jutted skyward from a rust-colored soil that in turn was intermittently carpeted in islands of vegetation splattered in dark yellow, jade, and auburn. He flew over this for several hours seeing nothing in the way of wildlife except for two small herd of springbok gazelle and a large sounder of warthog that he estimated 30 or more in number.

The flatness of the desert gave way to long, narrow draws filled with vegetation then to islands of mesquite and eucalyptus trees. Hills formed and these rose from the desert scrub in monuments of great rock, tangles of brush, and errant trees. Fences appeared and these not only marked property but served as guidelines for tall grasses and weeds, vines, and brush. Wildlife gave way to herds of cattle and soon the cows below him running through the desert scrub were those that grazed on his ranch.

He flew over the property and over livestock until he saw the collection of buildings that comprised his home. In addition to his house, there was the hangar where he housed the *Ruark*, a barn where he kept two trucks, a trailer, and other farm equipment, the pump house, and a small utility shed that was home to the controls for the ranch's wind turbines and solar arrays. He circled these then landed before the hanger. He powered down the craft and watched as the doors to the hanger opened. Xi walked out into the craft. Taylor exited.

"Come to welcome me back home?" Taylor joked knowing that Xi would shoot the question down with a snarky remark.

Xi waited until the blades of the *Ruark* came to a complete stop then walked forward.

"No, I came to check on the ship," Xi said, his reply coming via his voice box, his speech heavily robotic and digitized.

"Really?" Taylor questioned. "You didn't come out to see me?"

"No."

"Okay. Then could you please put her in the hanger and make sure she's ready for tomorrow. I'll be taking Lou back to Kai."

Xi nodded.

"Where is Lou by the way?" Taylor said, looking toward the house. "I thought she'd for sure come out to greet me."

"She's on the deck with Turner," Xi said.

"Turner Too, you mean," Taylor corrected. "Turner died."

"All dogs are the same," Xi huffed, his voice box making his disparaging remark seem even more exasperated.

"Respect the dogs," Taylor chuckled. "Past and present."

Xi ignored the comment and instead made his way to the *Ruark* to see to his assigned duties.

Taylor turned and left his Jack of all trades and only ranch hand to his perceived burdens and headed toward the house. He walked over the compacted soil of the area before the hangar then on to a lawn of freshly cut grass and finally to before the covered porch that surrounded his home. He saw Lou sitting with her legs beneath her on the couch reading a book. Turner Too stood from the chair she was balled into and stretched. She let out a deep yawn then bounded off the concrete deck and into the yard and before Taylor. She leaned into his legs while Taylor patted her.

"Love you too girl," Taylor assured his dog. The Rhodesian ridgeback's red pelage shinned in the afternoon sun. "You're a good girl."

Turner enjoyed the attention bathed upon her for another moment then bounded back onto the deck and into her chair.

Taylor followed. He stood at the bottom step taking in the woman before him. She was of Chinese descent and beautiful with porcelain skin and jet-black hair. She was dressed in a loose-fitting T-shirt and a pair of denim cutoff shorts. She was barefoot and wore no jewelry and little in the way of makeup. Her hair was piled high atop her head in a loose bun and held in place by two lacquer red chopsticks.

"You're back," Lou said without looking up from her book.

"That I am," Taylor replied.

He walked up the short set of stairs and to Lou's chair. He leaned over to kiss her. She received his kiss on the lips then returned to her book.

"Go shower," Lou almost sighed. "Get cleaned up then join me out here."

Taylor nodded.

Lou held her gaze in her book.

Taylor ignored the slight and instead ventured into the house. He passed through the trophy room and through its display of mounted animals taken all over Mars then past the open kitchen, and down the hall to the master bedroom. He removed his pistol and holster, and the knife and Taser derringer from his belt and placed them on the dresser. He removed his Kevlar wrist gauntlet's that held hidden retractable blades and placed these too on the dresser. He made his way to a reading chair in the corner of the room, sat, then took off his boots and socks. He stood and made his way across the room and into the master bath. He disrobed and got into a hot shower.

Much like he did in the *Ruark*, Taylor took advantage of his time alone by trying to calm himself.

"She's mad you saw Dej. She doesn't understand. She'll get over it."

Taylor let the shower wash his words down the drain then let the hot water run over his head. He did this for several minutes then exited and dressed. He put on a well-worn pair of khaki shorts and even older loose-fitting chambray shirt that he was forced to wear open at the front because it only had one button left. He went to the kitchen, opened two bottles of Tsing Tsao beer, and walked back to the patio. He handed Lou a beer then clanked his bottle against hers.

Lou looked up.

"What are we toasting?"

"How about...the afternoon."

Taylor took a long pull on his beer then sat in his chair that sat catty cornered to the couch.

Lou put her book down and took a drink. She turned slightly to look at Taylor. His short hair was still wet from the shower, and he needed to shave. But then he always needed to shave. The man lived under a permanent stubble.

"How is she?" Lou asked, her voice warm and sincere.

"Is that what you're mad about?"

"Who said I was mad?"

"Your actions."

Lou took a quick sip of her beer.

"I am mad but at you. I'm not mad at her."

"Good because she wouldn't know you are mad at her if you were."

Lou took on a look of disgust. Taylor took another pull of his beer.

"Don't talk about her like that," Lou finally blurted out.

Taylor took another drink.

"And I'm not talking about her," Lou reiterated. "I'm talking about you."

"What about me?"

"I'm worried about you," Lou confessed. She put her beer on the table beside her then leaned forward on the couch and toward Taylor. "I'm worried about you. Very worried."

"Why?" Taylor questioned, truly unsure of what she was referring to.

"The last thing you need to do is go see her."

Taylor started to speak.

Lou didn't let him.

"You have enough worries without going to see someone in..." Lou fumbled for the words. "In pain. Hurting. In a way that you can do nothing about."

"Worries?"

"Yes. Taylor, yes," Lou exclaimed. "Your past is catching up with you, baby. I think you have PTSD."

"PTSD?"

"From what happened to Dejah. Your time in the Corps. What you do for Shun."

Taylor had heard enough.

He killed his beer and stood.

"I'm going to grab another."

Lou reached out her hand. She took Taylor by the wrist and pulled him toward her.

"You have nightmares every night."

"I can live with that. I have for a long time."

6

———

Neva Grant adjusted the tinted goggles upon her face, pushed off the floating dock, and aimed towards the depth. The water was warm and gin clear and the visibility before her far past the point of being measured. She glided to the first cable of oysters that hung vertical before her, gave a quick directional kick of the long fins she wore, and slowly drifted down the column of shells. She looked at each shell to ensure it was unbroken and still flourishing in the nutrient rich waters that Mǔlì floated upon.

The community was small, encompassing only a few buildings, most of which stood to serve the oyster farm, the fishing and pleasure boats that occasionally came by for fuel or repairs, and / or the community as a whole. Roughly 60 full-time residents lived on the floating atoll, and these ranged in age from five to 68.

Neva was 17.

She reached the end of the long, glistening white shells, gently glided over to the next column and inspected them as she slowly kicked for the surface. She broke through to the air, took a breath, and dove back beneath the surface. Neva repeated this process of swimming down one string of oysters and up another 20 times before she heard the telltale sign of an approaching ship. She could tell by the depth of the propellor sound that the ship was large and that it was approaching quickly.

Neva came to the surface and made her way along the dock where she continued to the floating waystation. The city was crafted of recycled plastic, aluminum, steel, and corrugated tin. The compound more or less sat in a circle with dozens of long docks and boats slips spoking outward like tentacles reaching towards the sea. Neva pulled the goggles free from her face and swam to the ladder. She removed her fins and tossed them onto the landing along with her goggles. She climbed the ladder and onto the deck.

Mǔlì was bustling with men, women, and children. Perhaps 40 people milled about the atoll in the early morning sun playing, preparing for the day ahead, or sharing stories with one another. A small girl of about eight or nine stepped onto the dock. Neva's smile spread at the sight of her. The girl called to Neva and ran toward where she stood. Neva watched the child running to her and crouched in preparation to hug the girl upon her arrival.

A sharp whistle cried across the sky.

Neva looked up just as a four-story living quarter exploded outward in a shower of tin and wood. The blast blew Neva off the dock and into the water. She landed on her back and sunk 10 feet before she was able to right herself and swim upward. She broke the surface to see thick smoke billowing in the air. Neva powered forward and toward the ladder.

The air exploded into a cacophony of automatic gunfire and cries for help, small explosions, and screams of anger. Another explosion rocked the atoll. Orange flames shot upwards of 30 feet. Neva pulled herself partway onto the dock to see people running in every direction. She saw men of all races and creeds wearing blood-soaked body armor cutting their way through the civilian populace with rifles, pistols, spears, and machetes.

Neva ducked back into the water. She dove beneath the dock and swam underneath it and to the center of the atoll. She rose into an air pocket beneath the decking and peered through the slats above her. Dead and dying civilians littered the deck. Those that stood cowered at the armed mob approaching them. One man stood before the group. He was of Chinese descent, was balding with long black hair, and sported a long goatee. His face was smeared in sweat and soot. He looked the crowd over then turned back to his men.

"Take the women. Children. Kill the rest."

The populace of the Mŭlì started to object. Those that weren't women or children never had their voices heard.

Gunfire erupted.

7

Taylor hated Enos.

He hated the way he spoke, his demanding yet passive aggressive demeanor, and his expectations of the proper use of a comm.

"Are you there, Taylor?" Enos asked. "I can't see you. Can you see me?"

Taylor looked over at Lou who had her hand plastered to her mouth in an attempt not to laugh. She was well aware of Taylor's disdain for Enos and took enjoyment watching Taylor writhe in anger while he spoke to him.

"That's because my hologram projector is off," Taylor groaned.

"Is it broken?"

"No!" Taylor barked. "I'm piloting the _Ruark_. Watching your hologram or shooting one of me while I fly is the last thing I need to be doing."

"I see," Enos said before realizing he'd inadvertently made a joke and burst into faint laughter. "Actually, I don't see."

Lou further plastered her hand against her mouth. Her eyes squinted tight, and she shook in an attempt to stifle her laughter.

Taylor tightened his grip on the controls of his ship. He gritted his teeth and slightly shook his head from side to side.

"What do you want, Enos?" Taylor snapped.

The sound of Enos clearing his throat echoed over the *Ruark's* overhead speaker.

"Shun would like to see you tomorrow."

"I'm flying into Kai and will be staying at the hotel tonight," Taylor interrupted.

"Good," Enos replied. "Would tomorrow morning at nine be acceptable?"

"Yes. I'll see you then," Taylor barked before abruptly ending the call with a flick of a switch.

Lou burst into heavy laughter and Taylor screamed in feigned anger.

The couple reached Kai shortly before sundown. They made their way from the airfield to Taylor's apartment at Biānjìng House. They settled in, made love, showered, and changed for a night on the town. They first went to The Forked Tongue, an upscale club that catered to Kai's small upper class, wealthy criminals, those in town on business, and those looking to take advantage of the aforementioned. The couple was seated at a table for two on the balcony that over-looked the main bar and the dance floor below. They shot Red Crowe tequila and drank beer chasers and watched the crowd below and laughed and enjoyed themselves.

They took a late dinner at the Ocean Club on the other side of town then made their way back to Taylor's where they again made love then fell asleep in each other's arms.

8

———————

Shun's meeting room was massive in stature and grand in collection. The artifacts found within the trophy room hailed from dynasties and empires long past on Earth and on Mars. Rugs woven of fantastic colors by craftsmen long since dead covered almost every inch of the stained concrete floor while art formed in countless mediums adorned the walls and sat upon several stands.

The double doors opened two minutes before nine and Shun entered, followed closely behind by his assistant, Enos.

Shun was dressed in tan slacks, brown crocodile loafers, and in a rose-colored loose-fitting linen shirt. His skin was tan and his thick smoke gray hair permanently slicked back against his head. He walked to Taylor, smiled, and held out his hand.

"Taylor, as always, good to see you."

The men shook hands.

"Good to see you as well," Taylor offered.

Shun gestured toward a pair of leather club chairs. The two men sat facing each other. Ennis carried a cigar humidor over to Taylor. Taylor took a cigar from the mahogany box and cut it without looking to the man who just presented it to him.

"Good to see you, Taylor," Enos joked. "To actually see you."

"Uh huh," Taylor groaned.

Enos' face took on a look of hurt.

Shun took a cigarette from a silver case on the table to his left, lit it, and drew in a lungful of smoke. Taylor lit his cigar and eased back in his chair.

"How is the ranch?" Shun politely inquired.

"As remote and beautiful as ever," Taylor answered.

"Just as you like it," Shun commented with a slight smile.

Taylor nodded.

Shun took another drag on his cigarette, exhaled, eased back in his chair, and crossed his legs.

"Taylor," Shun began anew. "A friend of mine has a dilemma and has asked my assistance in dealing with such. I'd like you to handle the situation."

"Yes sir. Of course," Taylor replied.

"Several of Kantar Saber's interest have been decimated."

"Kantar Saber?" Taylor both repeated and interrupted. He leaned forward in his chair in interest.

"Yes. His information has been sent to your comm," Enos said from his place behind Shun.

Taylor was well aware of who Kantar Saber was and of the power he held. He controlled everything upon, under, and bordering the Great Northern Sea. He was one of the most powerful officers in the Martian Triad. Taylor couldn't imagine what type of dilemma Kantar was facing or why he couldn't handle it himself. The man was notoriously ruthless.

Shun explained that Kantar came to him for assistance as he feared whoever was striking out against him could possibly be one of his own men.

"Kantar asked that we find those responsible for his losses and bring them before him," Shun added.

"Again, all the details have been sent to your comm," Enos explained.

"I'll need some help for something this big," Taylor announced.

Shun nodded in agreement.

"Of course. Assemble whatever you need. However you handle this is up to you."

"Might I suggest Arnie Molen," Enos said. "He's in our employment and considered to be one of the top technology specialists on the planet."

"Send me his contact," Taylor instructed.

Enos nodded that he would.

"Well then," Shun said as he stood, "please keep me informed."

9

─────────

The Rat Hole was one of the most notorious bars in all of Kai and the only one to feature a live gorilla that favored eating rats. The gorilla was a massive beast standing more than 10 feet tall and weighing 600 pounds. His hair was salt-and-pepper gray in color and his eyes glazed in milky cataracts. The ancient ape lived in a pit below the bar and did little in the way of activity except during feeding time when it was thrown a knot of rats to feast upon. Customers bet on which rats would be devoured first and in what order. Taylor had first visited The Rat Hole a decade earlier with his friend, Joel.

Taylor didn't frequent the bar often and hadn't been inside its doors in over a year. The first thing he noticed upon entering the establishments was the rank smell of the gorilla. Even over the cigarette, cigar, and hash smoke, the reek of body odor and sweat, the ape's musty, musky odor was strikingly apparent. The pungent smell reminded Taylor of the bonobos he had encountered on an assignment in the equatorial jungles near Reisman.

He had heard of the chimps and how they had entered the Stone Age and were proficient with spears and bows and arrows by one of his guides. Taylor hadn't believed his guide at the time but saw the living proof and was attacked by such in the days that followed.

Taylor pushed through the smells and past the small crowd of people to the elongated bar. He found an opening between customers and dropped some cash on the bar. An obese man on the other side of the bar waddled towards Taylor. He looked at the cash on the counter then back to Taylor.

"What?" the bartender snapped.

"Beer," Taylor replied.

The man nodded, took the cash, and waddled away. He returned a moment later with a tall glass of beer. He put it on the counter, Taylor took it, and pulled a long drink.

"Not as warm as the last one I had in here," Taylor exclaimed.

"Yeah, we got a new cooler a month ago," the bartender proudly exclaimed as he waddled away from Taylor and toward a woman leaning over the far end of the bar.

Taylor took another drink then turned to gaze over the populace.

The customers of The Rat Hole were a collection of workers covered in filth, soldiers in tattered and well-worn uniforms, mercenaries, criminals, ex-cons, prostitutes, and pimps. All looked drunk or stoned or both or in the process of getting such and were armed with pistols, rifles, or knives. Most were smoking and all were drinking.

A tall man of about 6' 5" and carrying 285 pounds of hard-sculpted muscle cut through the crowd and toward Taylor. The man wore his brownish blonde hair and a flat top and was dressed in worn body armor. He carried a pistol on each side of his hips.

"Taylor!" the man exclaimed, thrusting out his hand. "It's been a while."

Taylor gripped Eric Kavanaugh's hand in his and exclaimed, "That it has, Kav."

The two men sized each other up making note of how the other carried himself and of how age had treated them.

"Come on," Kav exclaimed. "I got a table in the back. We can talk there."

Taylor nodded and followed Kav through the crowd to a table of rough plywood and four mismatched chairs. The men sat opposite one another and Kav yelled through the crowd to a young waitress.

"Sam!"

The waitress turned around to reveal that she was a Descendant. Her face was palsied and drooping in folded skin. She approached the table.

"What you need, sugar?" she asked of Kav.

"Couple shots of Red and two beer chasers," Kav replied.

The waitress nodded and turned. Kav grabbed her wrist and spun her back around.

"And then two more shots and two more beers after that. Keep them coming."

Kav let the waitress free, and she nodded with a slight smile, and walked away. He pulled a cigarette from a pocket behind his plate carrier and lit it. Taylor did the same with a cigar. The waitress returned, placed two shots of Red Crowe tequila and two glasses of beer on the table, turned and left. The men toasted shots, slammed them, then each took a sip of beer.

"Same old piss warm beer," Kav exclaimed.

"Bartender says they just got a new cooler," Taylor said.

"Bartender's full of shit. Always has been."

Taylor gave a small laugh. He took another pull on his beer then cut to the chase.

"I've got a job."

"That's why I'm here," Kav replied.

"Kantar Saber," Taylor said. "Somebody's been hitting him hard."

"That somebody's got big balls, is a dumb ass, or has a hell of an army backing 'em up!" Kav exclaimed. "Going after Kantar, I mean, damn. God damn."

"Yep," Taylor took a long drag on his cigar. "Whoever it is took out several ships, two communities, and a Sulphur plant."

"What's he doing?"

"Hits them hard. Takes women and children…"

"Sex slavery?" Kav interjected.

"Probably," Taylor replied.

"What else?" Kav asked.

"That's it. They take women. Children. Nothing else. Have killed everyone else they encountered."

"Then how do you…"

"They've always left one survivor…"

"Someone to tell the tale."

"They've sunk ships with millions worth of cargo and sent communities to the bottom of the sea."

The waitress returned and placed four more drinks on the table. Taylor and Kav killed their beers, and the waitress took their empties. The duo slammed their tequilas then moved on to their new beers.

"I gotta say," Kav paused midsentence to light a fresh cigarette. "None of that makes a damn bit of sense."

"We don't have to understand it. Just stop it," Taylor exclaimed on a cloud of smoke. "I'd go crazy if I tried to make sense of half the things Shun has me do."

"You still working for Shun?" Kav asked.

"For the rest of my life," Taylor replied.

Kav took a long drag on his cigarette then exhaled.

"Shun," Kav halfway scoffed. "He makes Kantar Saber look like a kitten. Talk about ruthless. Rumor is that Shun's not just an officer in the Triad but that he *is* the Triad. That he runs the whole damn planet."

Taylor sat stoic.

Kav continued, "Thing I don't get is, as powerful as he is why does he live in a shit hole like Kai?"

Taylor drank his beer ignoring Kav's speculation about his boss. It wasn't that Taylor didn't believe what Kav was saying.

He did.

It just was none of his business.

Taylor worked for Shun because he made a deal with him over a decade ago. That deal was brokered on a foundation of trust and mutual respect. Taylor intended to keep that trust.

Kav could tell Taylor wasn't interested in his thoughts on Shun. He took another long pull on his beer and lit another cigarette.

"So, what's the plan," Kav asked, redirecting the conversation.

"Put together a team then head to sea," Taylor explained. "Bring all this bull shit to a head."

"How many you thinking?"

"Small group. Maybe four to five."

"Including me?"

"Including you."

Kav nodded and enjoyed his smoke.

"You got anyone else signed up?" Kav asked.

"Not yet," Taylor admitted. "Why? You know someone?"

Kav smirked.

"I might know a guy."

10

———

The Quarry made The Rat Hole look like a palace.

Located on the outskirts of town and close to the city airfield, the bar consisted of several shipping containers, chairs crafted from discarded wooden pallets, and tables made from scrapped aircraft parts. The shipping containers were open on two sides and through these windows was served beer and liquor, dope, and hash. The real appeal of The Quarry was a sandpit where fights of every kind were witnessed by those standing or sitting on crude bleachers. Fights were heavily bet upon and ranged in participants from dogs, hyenas, rats, monkeys, and humans. Taylor and Kav had come to the bar to watch a friend of Kav's fight.

Taylor and Kav each grabbed a beer and made their way through a crowd of working-class people, roughnecks, soldiers, loners, prostitutes, and rabble of every kind to the pit. They wove through the seated crowd to the top row of the bleachers and sat. The air was hot and dry and reeked of body odor, smoke, and open sewage.

An obese black woman entered the pit through a space between two sets of bleachers. She was followed by two fighters.

"Which one's Mark?" Taylor asked, gesturing towards the duo.

"The shorter of the two. The one smoking a cigarette," Kav exclaimed, while pointing at his friend. "He's not as small as he looks. That other guy's a freaking giant. Word is that his father was Descendent."

The black woman pulled a handheld microphone from between her enormous breasts. She held it to her lips and shouted to the crowd.

"Are you ready for a beat down?"

The crowd cheered.

The announcer shook her head in disappointment.

"I said, are y'all ready for an epic bareknuckle beatdown?"

The crowd responded with jeers and cheers.

"Then here we go!" the announcer exclaimed.

She pointed to Mark.

"Tonight's fight features a true hero of the Martian Corps. The recipient of three Purple Hearts, two Bronze Stars, and one questionable dishonorable discharge. He stands 5' 11" tall and weighs in at a tight 192 pounds. You know him. You love him. Mark Donavan."

Donavan stepped forward and into the center of the sand pit. He raised his hands in triumph and walked to the announcer and smacked her on her large posterior. The announcer smiled and growled like a cat in heat into her microphone.

"Promising to beat the ever-loving shit out of Donavan is a giant of a man who's no stranger to The Quarry." The announcer pointed to the gargantuan standing at the edge of the ring. "He stands 6' 7" tall, weighs over 340 pounds. He served in the Martian Corps before being sentenced to three years hard labor in the stockade. He's been out for over a year and fighting here every week. Give it up for Sargent Drudge."

The crowd exploded in screams of joy and excitement.

"Are we ready?" the announcer cried.

The crowd enthusiastically screamed that they were.

"Do we know the rules?" the announcer belted out.

"There are no rules!" the crowd bellowed back in unison.

"You damn right about that!" The announcer laughed. She collected herself then asked, "Have you placed your bets?"

The audience screamed that they had and held up slips of paper, or cash, or their comms to show that they had placed bets or were about to. The announcer backed out of the center of the ring. The two men stood at the ready at opposite sides of the pit. Both removed their shirts and tossed them aside. Donavan took one last drag on his cigarette then flicked the butt across the ring at Drudge. The monstrosity growled at the action and began repeatedly pounding his fist into his open palm.

"You're a dead man!" Drudge promised. "Dead!"

The announcer reached the edge of the pit.

"Let's fight till there's no more fight in you!" the announcer howled.

The crowd went crazy.

Drudge exploded forward and toward his opponent. Donavan made ready and met Drudge with a quick right hook. Drudge ignored the hammer blow and took Donavan's throat into his hands and lifted him off the ground. Donavan's leg swung in search of purchase. He grabbed Drudge's wrists. Drudge cackled in utter delight as Donavan's face grew beet red.

"Just watch," Kav said to Taylor.

Donavan balled his fists and drove them into Drudge's ears. The giant stumbled slightly. Donavan boxed Drudge's ears twice more and the monster of a man fought to keep his footing. Donavan pulled pack his hands and licked his fingers then grabbed the giant's ears. Donavan searched then drove his saliva slicked fingers into the gargantuan's ear canals as far as he could push them. Drudge howled in agonizing pain. He dropped Donavan and held his hands over his ears and screamed. Donavan backed up, took a deep breath, then kicked Drudge in the balls. The giant of a man leaned over at the waist in pain. Donavan kicked him in the face. Drudge fell forward and onto the ground. He rolled over and Donavan met him with a punch to the throat. Drudge grabbed his neck and flayed wildly in an attempt to breathe.

"He's gone! Done!" the announcer proclaimed of Drudge. She rushed forward and held Donavan's hand aloft. "Tonight's winner!"

The crowd screamed, some in elation and others in major disappointment. Cash was passed about and tickets torn in disgust. A duo of men dragged Drudge over the sand and out of the pit.

"Come on," Kav said to Taylor. "Time for an introduction."

11

———

Taylor looked up from the outdoor picnic table he shared to see Donavan and a young lady making their way through the crowd toward them. The woman was tan and thin. She stood 5' 7" and had short jet-black hair. Like Donavan, she was wearing body armor, was heavily armed, and smoking a cigarette.

"Hell of a fight, man," Kav offered.

The two men shook hands. Kav and the woman hugged in friendship.

Taylor stood.

"Taylor, this is Mark Donovan."

The men shook hands.

"Call me Donovan."

Taylor nodded in agreement.

"And this is Ruby," Donovan added, gesturing to the woman at his side.

Taylor held out his hand. Ruby took it.

"Ruby?" Taylor asked.

"It's Ruby Padron. Call me Ruby. I left the whole last name bull shit when I got outta the Corps."

Taylor nodded again.

"Ruby it is."

The four sat and Kav handed the two guests beers. Both nodded in appreciation and drank.

"I'll get right to the start, Donovan," Kav started anew. "I just signed on for a job with Taylor. And he's looking for another hand. I recommended you."

Donovan nodded and looked at Taylor.

"What's the job?" he asked.

"Somebody or someone's been hitting Kantar Saber's territory," Taylor said. "We're gonna find them."

"Kantar Saber!" Ruby exclaimed. "That's one bad ass son of a bitch. I heard he once skinned a guy. Alive."

"No," Donovan interrupted. "He once skinned a guy while that guy's wife was forced to watch."

"That's not our concern," Taylor exclaimed. "My job is to find who's hitting his ships. Kav told me about you. I pulled your military records. Seen you fight. You in?"

"What's the pay?" Ruby questioned.

Taylor shot Ruby a puzzled look. Donovan intervened.

"We're a pair. We work together."

"I'm not taking on a romantic couple."

Ruby laughed.

"We're not a couple. I don't even play on his team."

Taylor thought on Ruby's comment for a moment then understood.

"What's your background?" Taylor asked of Ruby.

"The woman retrieved a comm from the pocket behind her plate carrier and opened and app. She worked the display then spoke.

"Military records just sent to your comm. I got out three years back. Done freelance ever since."

"Most of that work with me," Donovan added. He looked to Taylor. "You hire me, you hire her."

The crowd milling around the table parted.

"Cheating son of a bitch!"

Drudge drove for Donovan.

Ruby leapt upon the table and delivered a lightning-fast blur of a spinning roundhouse kick to Drudge's jaw. The giant's head jerked sideways. His body followed, twisted, and collapsed backward into the ground. Ruby dropped from the table and to Drudge's side. He fought to stand. She delivered a kick to the side of his head that rolled him over and into unconsciousness.

Ruby took her beer from the table, killed it, and exclaimed, "I need another."

12

Lou usually enjoyed working the morning shift at Biānjìng House.

The hotel was lonely at that time of day with most guests having left earlier for meetings or sleeping in from having too much fun the night before. Lou enjoyed the freedom from guests and used the time to clear her mind. She enjoyed the tranquility.

This morning was different.

This morning she stood at the guest relations counter thinking of Taylor and, more importantly, of her relationship with him. She worried about him. He drank heavily, smoke cigars almost constantly, and got almost no rest. When he did rest, his sleep was interrupted by dreams painted in violence and regret. These were born of his feelings that the death of his parents and the almost catatonic state his first love lived in were his fault.

This was foolish, of course, but it was what he believed.

This combined with his time in the Corps and his years of service to Shun made for a man nearing the breaking point. Whether or not this was the reason he had failed to take their relationship to the next level she didn't know. She only knew that she loved him greatly and that he didn't love her the same way.

Otherwise, he would change his life and they would be married.

The hotel security guards opened the front doors and a woman entered. Lou came from around the counter and stood ready to greet her.

The woman that walked from the double doors was tall, standing 5' 8". She had white-blonde hair that was shorn on the sides. Her body armor was formfitting and only accentuated a stunning figure and ample bust.

The lady walked to Lou.

"Good morning," Lou began. "Welcome to Biānjìng House. How may I be of service?"

Lou found the woman even more attractive close up. Her skin was porcelain smooth and her eyes strikingly grayish blue.

"I'm looking for a man I believe is a guest here. Jack Taylor."

Lou's jaw tightened at the mention of her boyfriend's name.

The woman seemed to notice.

Lou quickly smiled.

"Do you have a room number?"

"No, I..."

"I'm sorry. I can't reveal the names of our guests. If you knew for certain that he was staying with us—"

"I know he lives here. Part-time."

"Then you have his room number?"

"No."

"Then I'm afraid..."

The woman pulled a comm from a pocket behind her chest plate.

"Look. I know he lives here when he's not out on the frontier or on assignment."

Lou began to speak.

The woman swiped the screen of her comm.

"I just sent you my contact info. Please share them with Mr. Taylor when he's next in. That's all I ask."

Lou reluctantly gave a slight nod, one that she felt neither confirmed nor denied that her boyfriend lived at the hotel.

The woman turned and left. Lou returned to behind the counter. She opened the message on her comm and read the name aloud.

"Ravaa."

13

———————

Arnie Molan swiped his card in front of the door to his suite and entered. The door shut behind him. He walked down the hall and into the living area. The room was bleak and sterile and was furnished in modern furniture crafted from black leather, concrete, and chrome.

He made his way to the center of the room to notice candles burning on all the side tables. They smelled of jasmine.

An adjoining door opened, and an insanely voluptuous woman entered the room. She wore a black corset, panties, and thigh-high stockings. Her black hair was flared and cascaded over her shoulders in waves. Her lips were painted cherry red.

She sashayed forward and into the room. Her black stilettos clicked on the concrete floor. She stopped just short of Arnie. He found her perfume intoxicating. The woman jutted her hip outward to the side and ran her hands seductively down her body.

"What's the matter, baby?" she purred. "Cat got your tongue?"

A male voice called from the beyond.

"Arnie? Arnie, are you there?"

Arnie moaned. He finger punched the controller on his wrist and his coal black contact lenses returned to being transparent. He adjusted his eyes and looked to the hologram on the table before him.

"Yes, Enos," Arnie answered. "I'm here."

"I hope I'm not disturbing you."

Arnie pulled the small patch from below his nose that allowed him to smell in Alter World and placed it in his wrist controller.

"No. I'm free," Arnie lied. "Wasn't doing anything important."

Enos nodded.

"I need you to contact Jack Taylor," Enos continued. "I've sent you his information. Let me warn you that he will not answer via hologram."

Arnie's brow scrunched in confusion.

"Who is..."

"Mr. Taylor is an associate of Shun's. He will be leading a team to assist in the capture of some undesirables who have been attacking an associate's dealings on the Great Northern Sea."

"The Great Northern...like the ocean?" Arnie sputtered.

"Yes."

"I...I don't like water. That's why I live in the middle of the desert."

Enos sighed.

"What did I tell you about disappointing Shun?"

"Uh...Not to."

"That is correct."

Arnie eased back in his seat defeated.

Enos continued, "Mr. Taylor will undoubtably need technical assistance while on assignment and given the belief that the attackers are using some sort of stealth tech..."

Arnie shot upward in his seat suddenly interested.

"Stealth tech!" he exploded. "What kind?"

"You will be fully briefed..."

"Tell me something!" Arnie shot back. "I mean, this is huge. Stealth tech on Mars?"

"A survivor from the long liner *Aurora*, a man by the name of Hall said the ship that attacked him sat behind a shimmering cloud. That it simply appeared as boil of heat. A mirage of some sort."

"That's far more than stealth," Arnie excitedly burst.

"Yes. You will get to ask Mr. Hall about it yourself. But first..."

"But first I need to contact Taylor. Got it. On it."

14

"Who's Ravaa?"

Taylor entered the door to his apartment and dropped his knapsack on the floor. He walked to Lou and kissed her. She reluctantly received it.

"Glad to be home," Taylor said.

Lou held the look of anger on her face.

"I asked you, who's Ravaa?"

Taylor took a Tsing Tao beer from the small refrigerator next to his desk and opened it.

"I don't know," Taylor calmly confessed. He, of course, could tell that Lou was angry and upset but he refused to engage her in an argument just for argument's sake. "Who is she?"

"She's the hot little bitch that came in here looking for you today. She says she knows you live here."

"I don't know her."

"Then how does she know you live here?"

Taylor sat on the couch and upended his beer.

"I don't know," Taylor answered. "What does she want?"

"You! That's it," Lou angrily retorted. "She asked for you and sent her contact info to my comm."

Taylor stood and walked to Lou.

"Let me see," Taylor said.

Lou held her comm out in front of her and swiped open an app. A hologram of Ravaa's face appeared above the comm. Taylor looked at it then studied it with interest.

"I don't know her," Taylor admitted. "But something about her looks... Familiar."

Taylor continued his study the hologram.

"What's in the attachment?" Taylor asked.

"What?"

"The attachment?"

"I didn't open..." Lou stopped midsentence and opened the attachment. It was a military record. Taylor scanned it. It showed Ravaa entering the Corps at 18 and racking up a ton of accolades before exiting at 27.

Taylor returned to the couch and took a drink of his beer.

"Probably looking to join the team I'm putting together."

"What team?"

"I need some help on an assignment."

Anger seemed to radiate from Lou. Taylor gave up.

"What is wrong?" he asked. "And it's not somebody looking for me, probably trying to land a job."

Lou took a glass of wine from a side table and sat in the chair opposite Taylor.

"It's what we talked about the other night."

Taylor was lost. He had no idea what conversation she was referring to.

"What?" he finally asked.

"You don't remember?"

Taylor did his best not to sigh in disbelief at her question or at her attitude.

"I guess not," Taylor reluctantly admitted.

"I'm worried about you."

"You don't need to be."

"I think you have PTSD."

"I don't."

"I want you to see someone. I want you to change your ways."

"Change my ways?"

"Quit doing things that only aggravate your condition like," Lou searched frantically for the words. "Like working for Shun. Like seeing Dejah."

"Enough!" Taylor's voice was sudden and stern.

Lou shot back in her chair. She'd never seem Taylor short with her. She wasn't going to let him get away with it. She collected herself and returned to outlining her beliefs.

"Do these things…"

Taylor stopped her short.

"I'm warning you, don't give me ultimatums."

"Do these things…or I may not be here when you get back."

Taylor calmly stood.

"Don't give me ultimatums," he said again, this time slow and drawn. "Whether you leave or not's your choice."

Taylor walked to the door.

Lou jutted upward from her chair.

"Where are you going?" she cried.

"To work."

Taylor exited his apartment and made his way to the stairs and down to the lobby and then onto the street outside the hotel.

"Taylor," a voice called.

Taylor turned to see a striking woman. His mind raced to where he had seen her before.

"You're…" Taylor started.

"Ravaa," the woman finished.

15

"Ray Va."

Taylor nodded in understanding and repeated the name back to the woman sitting across from him then asked her last name.

"No last name. Just Ravaa."

A waitress appeared and she set two tequila two beers on the table. Taylor paid the waitress and raised his glass to Ravaa without saying anything. She mirrored his action and drank.

Taylor took a cigar from a pocket behind his plate carrier, cut it, and lit it. Ravaa did the same although with a much smaller cigarillo.

"Like I said," Ravaa began anew, "I'm looking for work. Steady if available."

Taylor exhaled a large cloud of smoke and took a drink of his beer.

"How did you know I was looking for crew?"

"Word's on the street."

"What's the street say about you?"

Ravaa smirked then took a drag on her cigarillo.

"That I'm good. Real good."

Taylor laughed and drank.

"Your military records are impressive. That's for sure. But what have you been doing since you exited?"

Ravaa took another puff on her cigarillo.

"Headhunting for an outfit out of Asann'e. I could give you the name of the guy I worked for but considering he was killed by his competition, I doubt you'd get much of a reference out of him."

"Bounty hunting?"

Ravaa nodded.

"Leashed over 108 my last year of employment."

"How many of those were brought in alive?"

"All the ones I was told to keep alive."

Taylor drank his beer while mulling over the woman across from him. Ravaa was a fantastic soldier, had earned a number of accolades during her time in the service, and by her own admission, wasn' afraid of hard and somewhat suspect work. She was confident and her body armor and the two pistols she carried on her hips showed that she was knowledgeable about the best in gear and weaponry.

Taylor held his gaze trying not to stare. Something about her looked familiar. He felt he'd seen her somewhere before but for the life of him, he couldn't place her.

He decided to take a chance.

"We ship out tomorrow," Taylor explained. "Can you be ready by then?"

Ravaa up ended her beer.

"I'm ready now."

16

The hangar where Taylor kept the *Ruark* while in Kai was an ancient structure crafted of steel and concrete. Its outside was stained in rust and city pollutants and scarred from years of neglect and battles with multiple sandstorms. Inside the hangar was a flurry of activity. Beneath a few naked bulbs that hung from the ceiling, Taylor and his team checked and rechecked hard plastic cases filled with equipment ready to be loaded into the chopper.

Taylor stepped to the gun vault case before Kav.

"Eight HK Urban Assault Viper rifles. Four 30 round magazines each. Four hundred rounds of ammo in assorted flavors and colors," Kav said as he ran his hands over the rifles carefully nestled in cut foam channels.

Taylor checked what Kav said against the info logged in his comm and nodded.

"Load it up," Taylor said before moving on to Ruby and the open case before her.

"Two RK 17 Shoulder-Launched Multipurpose Assault Weapons," Ruby exclaimed. "Six rockets each. Heat seekers and slugs."

Taylor nodded, jerked his thumb in the direction of the *Ruark* and moved on to Donavan.

"What we got here is a plethora of things that go bang," Donavan joked. "Two dozen flash grenades, one dozen pepper spray grenades, and two dozen good old-fashioned blow shit up grenades."

Taylor smiled at Donavan's enthusiasm and said, "Fun times to be had for sure. Load them up."

Taylor next moved to Ravaa and the narrow case before her.

"Two Daniel Defense rifles each mounted with Swarovski 3 – 10 x 42 scopes and six boxes of bullets. Three ammo piercing. Three ballistic."

Taylor nodded.

Ravaa closed the gun case and moved to a deep square case to her side.

"Six pairs of tactical contact lenses and wrist controllers," Ravaa looked to Taylor and smiled then returned to the box before her. "This is bad ass. I don't know where you get your gear, but this shit is top notch."

"I have a personal shopper," Taylor joked. "Gets me everything I need."

Ravaa then picked up a box of lenses. "I used night vision back in the Corps on a few assignments, but these are dual. Night vision and thermal plus magnification. Very nice."

"Yes, they are," Taylor agreed. "Get them on board."

Taylor walked to a table upon which Arnie had four open cases. Taylor looked in the boxes to see that he recognized almost nothing of the electronics presented before him.

"What is all this shit?" Taylor asks.

A huge smile stretched across Arnie's face. He began to speak. Taylor cut him off.

"Is this everything you need?"

"Yes. I've got..."

"I'll take your word for it. Load it up."

"You don't want me to..."

"No."

Taylor turned to the remainder of his team.

"We loaded?" he asked.

Ravaa answered, "Yes sir. We are. All good and ready to go."

"Then let's do it," Taylor announced.

A few last-minute items were thrown in the chopper and the team loaded up.

"You mind if I take the copilot seat?" Ravaa asked Taylor as they made their way toward the ship.

Taylor took the unlit cigar from his mouth to answer, "Sure," he said. "But you ain't flying her."

"Don't worry," Ravaa said with a smile. "I'm not fond of antiques."

"Antiques!" Taylor shot back with a laugh. "Try classic. She's a classic."

The team loaded into the craft and Taylor brought her to life. He lifted up and out of the hanger then climbed to 6,000 feet and flew north. The *Ruark* soared over the outskirts of Kai and over the hard-scrabble desert and over sections of land dissected by fence and barbed wire and cornered off pastures dotted with grazing cattle, horses, and camels. Taylor spotted a herd of springbok that numbered more than 50, and soon the shredded remains of one of these animals being devoured by a trio of condors.

The desert gave way to forests of eucalyptus and acacia and in the openings between the stands of these trees ran a half dozen species of antelope, blesbok, and the occasional bear.

"You always fly this low?" Ravaa asked of Taylor.

Taylor kept his eyes straight ahead.

"When I can. I like to see things."

"You from Mars?" Ravaa asked.

"Born and raised," Taylor replied. "How about you?"

"Born here," Ravaa said on a small laugh. "Can't say that I was raised here or by anyone."

Taylor nodded but didn't ask her to explain the comment.

The forest below stretched on, and they flew over this for several hours before the topography changed. Forrest gave way to grassland and upon these roamed herds of antelope and a few feral longhorn cattle. They flew over this landscape for several hours and watched as the landscape slowly but continuously changed. The sea of grass gave way to marshland and in turn to mangrove swamp the waters of which were bluish green and filled with life ranging from colony after colony of vibrantly colored birds to herds of deer that fed in the shallows. The swamp gave way to ranchland and the occasional small town and then to the outskirts of Aruna.

The seaside city was a kaleidoscope of colors. Every building was painted in bright white, vibrant blue, soft peach, or shocking orange. The streets were wide and lined with palm trees and shrubbery. This vision of the ideal beach community soon gave way to the harsh realities of the true industry of Aruna. The scenery below changed from homes and businesses painted in a cavalcade of colors to scrap and salvage yards, to landfills, open sewers, fields of rusty metal and cast-off machinery, and boat yards. The docks beyond this bustled with every kind of transport from small two-man crafts to commercial long liners.

Taylor banked the *Ruark* west and followed the coast. Commercial docks gave way to gravel beaches and dunes and ultimately to white sand beaches that stood immaculately raked and bright beyond belief. Ravaa checked the craft's location on a map that ran on the display screen between her and Taylor.

"We're on his property," Ravaa declared.

"You couldn't tell by the scenery below."

Ravaa ignored the comment and instead stared in awe at the paleaceous estate before her.

"That is one hell of a house," Ravaa exclaimed. "Damn. Thing's huge."

Taylor nodded and spoke into the ship's intercom.

"Prepare for landing."

Taylor brought the craft around and to a helipad that sat a safe distance from the main home. The *Ruark* landed and Taylor powered the craft down. All exited and immediately donned sunglasses in response to the blinding sun.

An open model SUV pulled up and two men exited. One was a

driver wearing body armor, dark shades, and a pistol on his thigh. The other man was tall and thin and well dressed.

Taylor stepped toward the man ahead of his team.

"Taylor," the man said. "I'm Chess, assistant to Mr. Kantar Saber. I thank you for coming."

Taylor nodded and the two men shook hands.

"I'll have some men assist you with unloading your gear and show you to your room shortly, but for now, Mr. Saber would like to meet you and your men."

Ravaa shot Chess a look.

Chess nodded and smiled.

"My mistake," Chess admitted. "Mr. Saber would like to meet you and your team."

"Sounds like a plan," Taylor said.

17

"His Excellency Kantar Saber, Eminence of the Great Northern Sea," Chess announced for all to hear.

Taylor bowed in respect. His team followed suit.

The group stood before Kantar as he held court from his couch. There was a trio of bodyguards to either side of him and two men sat in chairs next to the couch.

"Thank you for coming," Kantar bellowed. "And thank you in advance for bringing me those that have shown me such insult."

Taylor nodded and said that he and his team would do their best to ensure that just such a thing happened quickly.

Kantar gestured to one of the men seated next to him. The man stood.

"This is Hall. Ask him what you will," Kantar exclaimed on a thick cloud of hookah smoke.

The only survivor of the *Aurora* shyly stepped forward and to before Taylor and his team.

"Hall, I read your account of what happened," Taylor began. "But as it's been nearly a week since the attack, I was wondering if anything new has come to your mind."

"I told Mr. Saber and his men all I know," Hall exclaimed, his voice nervous and shaky.

"We know you did," Ravaa said. "It's just that sometimes an individual recalls something later once the initial shock of the event has subsided."

Hall thought for a moment.

"No. I told everything I...Katanga."

"What?" Taylor asked.

"I heard one of the men that attacked us call the leader of the group Katanga."

Kantar boiled in anger.

"Why are you just now telling this?"

Hall turned to face him, "I...I...just now remembered..."

"What else have you just now remembered?"

"That is...That is all, Your Excellency. I promise. I swear. The man's name was Katanga. That's all."

Kantar took in a heavy lungful of hash, then exhaled.

"Since you remember things when prompted by Taylor, I think it best you accompany him on his mission."

Hall shook in nervousness.

"Yes, sir...I wish to please you however I can."

Taylor thought of protesting the assignment then thought the better of it.

"Do you recall anything else?" Ravaa asked.

Hall turned around and shook his head.

"No," Hall answered nervously. "No...Nothing else."

The man who sat next to the chair Hall had vacated moments earlier stood. The man was short and stout and his facial features hinted at a mixed Chinese-American lineage.

"Taylor, I'm Capt. Bantu. You and your team will be stationed with me on the *Northern Butcher*."

The two men shook hands and Taylor introduced his team to the captain.

"Have to admit: I don't know that I like the idea of my ship and my crew being bait," Captain Bantu said to Taylor.

"You'll be bait regardless, until we catch whoever is doing this."

Captain Bantu accepted this fact with a nod of understanding.

Taylor continued, "Because of that, we'd like to get on board right away. The sooner we can outfit your ship, the sooner we can get to sea."

"I admire your enthusiasm," Kantar exclaimed on an exhale of thick hash smoke. "Let me know what you need."

"I will," Taylor replied. "And with your permission I'd like to start right away."

"Of course," Kantar said.

"Sir," Arnie shyly called out. "I mean, Your Eminence."

Kantar tilted his head in study of the young man addressing him. He looked far different than the others before him. Taylor and the rest of his group were strong, muscular, and intimidating. This man was different. He was small. Weak.

"Speak," Kantar said interested in what the small man had to offer.

"Is...Is that a monitor?"

Kantar looked to the massive lizard before his couch.

"Fred? Yes. He's my pet."

Kantar saw interest bloom across the man's face.

"Would you like to pet him?" Kantar asked, his voice calm and almost inviting. "He's asleep."

Arnie stepped forward.

"You sure?" Arnie asked, his voice cackling with childish excitement.

"Yes. Rub him behind the ears—where his ears would be if they stuck out. He likes that."

Arnie crept towards the monstrous lizard. He knelt gingerly and placed his right hand atop the reptile's head. The beast spun around and took Arnie's hand into his jaws and swung the man side to side. Arnie screamed in surprise and terror. Kantar and his bodyguards howled in laughter. Taylor and his team looked on in disbelief unsure of what to do. The lizard soon tossed Arnie aside. He came up on his knees on the verge of tears and gripping his right hand in his left. Ravaa ran to his side.

"Let me see it," Ravaa commanded.

Arnie reluctantly gave his hand. The extremity carried dozens of puncture wounds and was slicked in blood.

"You'll be fine," Ravaa said dropping Arnie's hand.

"I guess you patted him on the wrong spot," Kantar laughed.

18

The *Northern Butcher* was the premier whaling vessel upon the Great Northern Sea. She measured 420 feet in length, carried a 64 foot being, could reach speeds of 25 kn. She carried harpoon cannons both stern and bow and was operated by a seasoned crew of 25, not including the captain. Taylor and his team loaded the gear on board and took three small cabins. Taylor took the smallest of these, Ravaa and Ruby took another, Kav, Donavan, and Arnie took the third. Arnie set up his base of operation in the bridge, much to the disdain of Captain Bantu who found the heavily bandaged man annoying and intrusive.

"What is all this?" Bantu asked of what he saw as a mess of electronics upon a makeshift table Arnie set up.

"Basically, a monitoring station," Arnie replied.

"Monitoring? Monitoring what?"

"This one is the most important," Arnie explained, pointing to what looked like a laptop. "It allows me to monitor the anti-EMP I installed."

"EMP?"

"Electromagnetic pulse," Arnie explained. "A violent burst of energy that basically kills every electronic within a certain radius. Every attack on Kantar's property began with one."

"And what you've installed will protect the ship from such?"

"Yes."

"Good," Capt. Bantu said. "How much longer will you and your team need before we can set sail?"

"Another day at most," Taylor said upon entering the bridge. "Kav and Donavan are gonna run some lines under the ship."

"Lines?" Bantu asked.

"Air hoses and regulators?"

"What for?" Bantu asked puzzled by the idea.

"You never know," Taylor exclaimed.

19

O wen Riggs closed his laptop, took a clove cigarette from an open pack on the desk before him and lit it. He stood and walked out to the balcony of his penthouse on Star Island. The island and the community upon it were part of a sea steading operation that chose to be autonomous of any government. The community had enjoyed such for six months at which point representatives of Kantar Saber informed the community that they could dream of autonomy all they wanted but they would be paying for the privilege of being on the Great Northern Sea. The community agreed and made quarterly payments from that point forward without fail.

Fifteen hundred people lived on Star Island and their occupations ranged from the retired to fishermen to those that maintained the artificial island. Owen was the only writer to live on Star Island. His science fiction novels imagined a galaxy of adventures that featured interstellar travel, alien cultures, and worlds in need of rescue. The book sold well on both Mars and Earth and although Owen wasn't rich, his career did allow him to live where he chose.

He chose Star Island.

The community was affordable and allowed him plenty of fishing opportunities. Owen spent his mornings writing then broke for a cigarette or two before heading down to the docks to the artificial beach to try his luck for kingfish, shark, or mackerel.

Owen stood enjoying his clove cigarette on the balcony staring outward at the sea. It was a bright day and warm and the view from his perch on the fourth floor was awe-inspiring. The ocean was a vibrant blue, smooth as glass, and seemingly went on forever. Something in the vast blueness caught Owens' eye. Some 200 yards out was a patch of ocean that drew his attention. The section looked like a mere reflection of the area surrounding it. It shimmered like a mirage of some kind.

Owen was taken by a sudden silence. He dropped his cigarette into the ashtray on the table on the balcony and walked back inside. He noticed the lamp at the far side of the room was off. Likewise, the ceiling fan above. He walked to the control panel at the far wall and checked the display screen. It was dead and unresponsive. He walked into the kitchen and opened the refrigerator. The light didn't come on when he opened the door. The machine was dead.

The unexpected silence was interrupted by a series of loud pops. Owen returned to the balcony and to a scene of horror. A black ship sped toward the island. The cannon at the front of the ship flashed. A boom tore across the sea followed by a sharp whistle. Owen locked eyes on the fired object just as it slammed into the condo building next to his. The impact of the shell burst forth an explosion of flame and dust, concrete and steel. The percussion blast knocked him to the floor of the balcony. He grabbed the railing and pulled himself up to a standing position. He grabbed the railing and peered downward.

The black ship landed.

Men rushed from the craft, guns in hand and firing in every direction. Owen stood dumbfounded watching as men were gunned down in cold blood, women were knocked to the ground by rifle butts or with balled fists, and children were scooped up into arms offering anything but comfort or appreciation. The scene could have been torn from a battle in one of Owen's novels.

Something slammed into Owens' shoulder. The force of the hit knocked him backward and into the doorjamb. He reached to the pain in his right shoulder with his left hand and came away with a hand slicked in blood. He started to stand. A force unlike anything he'd ever felt before punched through his gut. The sensation was so strong and so sudden he lost control of his bladder and pissed himself. He gripped his gut in confusion and fear. He tried again to stand but his legs were too weak. A sudden wave of exhaustion washed over him. He couldn't keep his eyes open. His body called on him to sleep.

He fell over and to the floor and did just that.

20

———————

Ravaa exited the confined shower and dried herself with a towel that was far too small. She dressed in black pants and a gray-colored button-down shirt. She laced up her boots, pulled on her plate carrier vest, then fixed the holster to her leg. She checked her Sumners Arms 10 mm handgun, holstered it, then inspected her fixed blade knife and slid it into the sheath on her vest.

She exited the cabin and made her way toward the stairwell. Two men came from the door and into the hallway. The first man was short and stout with a face weathered by the elements and wore a gray beard that seemed to have never been washed. The man behind her was tall and thin and more or less clean-shaven.

The men walked forward and down the center of the hall. Ravaa stopped.

"Can I help you, miss?" the first man asked.

"No," Ravaa shot back.

She stepped to the side.

The man stepped in front of her.

"We're sure glad to see you and that other gal come on board," the man admitted, his voice low and dripping in sarcasm. "We don't get a lot of women on the *Northern Butcher*."

"I wonder why," Ravaa pondered, her voice as equally low and sarcastic.

"So, we were wondering if you'd like to visit for a time?"

Ravaa ignored the mans farfetched dream and began making her way past him. The man reached out and took Ravaa's wrist and spun her around.

"Hold on."

Ravaa's face tightened.

"You should have somebody look at that," Ravaa suggested.

"What?"

Ravaa grabbed the man by the back of his head and slammed his face into the wall. His nose collapsed, releasing a downpour of blood.

"Your nose. It looks out of sorts."

The taller man stepped aside and Ravaa made her way down the hall and up the stairwell to the main deck. She walked toward the bow to see Taylor and Captain Bantu watching the water below. Taylor turned to see her and hurriedly waved her over. Ravaa sped towards Taylor and he pointed to the sea below. Ravaa peered over the railing to see eight killer whales swimming in the ship's bow wave.

"They're beautiful," Ravaa exclaimed.

"And deadly," Captain Bantu offered. "Wolves of the sea."

Ravaa took on a look of interest.

Captain Bantu obliged her.

He told all he knew of the killer whales in terms of size and habits. He spoke of seeing a pack during a voyage 10 years past that numbered over 100. Of witnessing them hunt and how they had adapted to following whaling vessels knowing that where the ships went an easy meal in the form of a harpooned and incapacitated whale followed. Bantu shared the story of a mishap that occurred decades earlier when he was a harpooner on the *Roma*. Unlike the *Northern Butcher*, that ship was simply a whaler and not a factory ship. Therefore, the crew had to gut and butcher their kill on the sea and haul the smaller sections aboard.

"Fellow by the name of Tanner lost his balance and fell into the drink," Captain Bantu recalled. "Killer whale took him by the leg and shook that boy until muscle separated from bone. He was nothing but a sack of liquid by the time the whale tossed him aside."

"Tossed him aside?" Ravaa said in disbelief. "The whale did all that and didn't eat him?"

"No. Orcas just like to kill sometimes. They enjoy it."

Ravaa gazed upon the pod of black and white killers differently then watched as they skirted the wake and dove for the depths and out of sight.

Taylor took notice of this and of how the captain had merely observed the whales and asked if the species was ever targeted for harvest.

"Some smaller outfits hunt them for meat," Captain Bantu replied. "There's no real commercial value to them. Not like the leviathans we go after."

Ravaa's face once again took on a look of interest. She was out of her element on the ocean and was eager to learn anything she could about the very foreign Great Northern Sea.

Captain Bantu explained that leviathans were what sperm whales had become after the dead times. During that century at which the atmosphere thinned and radiation bathed the planet, the whales grew in size and strength. They mutated into the giants they were today. They were hunted for their meat, bones, hide, and oil. They were worth a fortune but hunting them wasn't for the frail of heart. It was a dangerous business that saw many lives lost annually in its pursuit.

"And that's before taking into account my ship and my crew being bait to catch who knows who. Or what," Captain Bantu said.

Taylor ignored the slight and instead stared ahead the Great Northern Sea before him.

21

"Hundred and fifty women worth a damn and about 90 kids."

Captain Katanga smiled at the news as delivered by his second in command Wang Lie. Star Island would turn quite a profit. The women and children would be sold into slavery and the money turned over to his boss.

Not that his boss was interested in money.

He wasn't.

He was seeking something else entirely.

Something Katanga didn't understand.

If he was after money, he wouldn't have ordered Katanga and his men to destroy all that they had encountered. Why he only took slaves and laid waste to the rest was a mystery to Katanga.

One he didn't question.

"Load them on the *Varro*," Katanga ordered. "Kill everyone else. Burn the city to its foundation."

Wang Lie nodded in understanding of his orders and left.

Katanga felt a small vibration in his chest. He pulled the comm from the shirt pocket behind his plate carrier and held it before him. The hologram that appeared above Katanga's comm showed a man hairless and burned. His skin was red and thin as paper. He wore an eye patch over his left eye and a black hard plastic mask covered his lower jaw and mouth. A myriad of tubes and wires ran from his mask and into some type of controls seemingly bolted to his chest.

"Katanga," the hologram declared.

"Yes, sir."

"You have a new target."

Katanga nodded in understanding.

"The *Northern Butcher* is a whaler out of *Aruna*," the hologram continued. "An old friend of mine is on board."

The hologram changed from the disfigured man to one of Taylor.

"Jack Taylor," the man's voice continued. "I want him alive. Bring him to me. Kill the rest. Sink the ship."

"Yes, sir."

22

Taylor, Ravaa, Kav, Ruby, and Donovan all stood at the stern of the *Northern Butcher*. Their gun cases sat open on the deck and a half dozen floating targets lined the railing behind them. The floats were crafted of industrial plastic and resembled an armed human figure as he might appear behind the railing of a boat.

Taylor pulled the comm from his pocket behind his vest and synced it to the first buoy.

"Who's up?" he asked of his team.

Ravaa stepped forward.

Taylor smiled. "Pistol then Viper then the Daniel Defense."

"Sounds good," Ravaa responded.

Donovan picked up one of the buoys and tossed overboard. The target sunk just below the surface of the water then exploded upward to bob up and down in the ship's wake. Ravaa stepped to before the railing, her pistol in hand.

"Damn!" Kav explained. "A custom."

"What can I say?" Ravaa said of her olive drab Sumners Arms 10 mm pistol. "I like to treat myself every now and again."

Taylor looked up from the display on his comm.

"Five yards," he said.

Ravaa raised her pistol and fired three times in quick succession.

"Two in the chest and one in the head," Donovan exclaimed. "Nice."

Ravaa lowered her pistol to her side.

"Ten yards," Taylor said.

Ravaa again raised her pistol and shot, putting another two rounds in the bobbing dummy's chest and one in the left side of its head.

"Nice," Ruby offered.

Ravaa holstered her pistol and walked to the case containing two HK Urban Assault Viper rifles.

"Eighteen yards," Taylor announced.

Ravaa leaned over the case.

"Forget the Viper. Let's see what that custom can do," Taylor chided.

Ravaa smirked and stood from the rifle case. She walked back to the railing.

"Twenty-two yards."

Ravaa stood watching the buoy bounce up and down further and further away.

"Twenty-six yards."

The team watched the buoy then looked to Ravaa. Some chuckled and all waited to see what would happen next.

"Thirty yards."

Ravaa drew her pistol and fired four times in lightning-fast succession.

"Holy shit!" Kav declared from behind a pair of binoculars. "All four in the head."

Ravaa smiled, blew over the top of her pistol's smoking barrel, and holstered her weapon.

"Think fast," Ruby warned.

Ravaa turned to see a Viper rifle flying through the air toward her.

"Thirty-seven yards."

Ravaa caught the rifle, turned, and unleashed a hail of automatic gunfire that literally decapitated the human-like target.

Taylor lit the cigar clenched between his teeth and declared, "Yep. He's dead."

Ravaa smiled and gave a quick laugh and the rest of the team joined in.

23

"I have to say, after seeing you all shoot today, I no longer feel like bait. I now feel like part of a plan. And I am honored that you are protecting me and my crew."

Captain Bantu raised his glass and Taylor, Ravaa, Kav, Donovan, and Ruby mirrored the gesture. Arnie was busy looking at his comm and so ignored the communion. Ruby put an elbow in his ribs and he quickly raised his glass to toast.

"To a quick success," Captain Bantu offered.

The group clinked glasses around the table and drank.

The dinner party was seated at a series of tables the captain had brought up on deck. They had just completed a dinner of grilled tuna steaks, roasted lemon potatoes, and fried green beans, and were now enjoying drinks and cigars or cigarettes under the stars.

"Well, I know we're on a mission, but I'm truly enjoying my time on board," Ruby declared to Captain Bantu and the rest of the table. "I've never seen the ocean like I have these past few days."

"It truly is the last frontier," Bantu exclaimed. "I learn something new about her every day."

"I've seen orca, porpoise, dolphin, fish galore, and sea birds in numbers I can't describe," Ruby continued. "When will we start seeing the leviathans you're after?"

"Any time," Captain Bantu said on a puff of cigar. "We crossed over into The Depths yesterday."

"The Depths?" Ravaa both repeated and asked.

"The Great Northern Sea isn't nearly as deep as the oceans on Earth. The area we crossed into is a mile to a mile and a half deep."

"That's not deep?" Ruby asked in disbelief.

"Not compared to Earth, no," Captain Bantu replied.

"Mars does beat Earth for deepest ocean trench however," Arnie announced. "The Mariana Trench on Earth is seven miles deep. The Northern Cut on Mars is eight and a half miles deep."

"And God knows what's down there," Captain Bantu pondered aloud. "As much as the Dead Times warped life on this planet, there could be true sea monsters down there for all man knows."

The group laughed and speculated at what lurked in the depths beneath where they sat. They continued enjoying their libations and told stories of times past near or on the water.

Taylor told of deep-sea fishing with his father when he was younger and of landing a blue Marlin that measured 14 feet in length and weighed over 2,100 pounds.

"Caught a baby then?" Captain Bantu joked.

Taylor laughed and said that he was only 14 at the time and he thought the fish a beast.

"They can get twice the size," Captain Bantu offered. "Or can. I once..."

A heavy moan carried through the air. All but Captain Bantu looked around for the source of the haunting cry.

The moan repeated.

"What is that?" Kav asked, still looking around.

"You won't see them," Captain Bantu warned. "Until it's too late."

Kav edged forward in his seat. Donavan and Ruby followed suit.

"Won't see what until it's too late?" Kav asked.

Captain Bantu took a long drink then puffed his cigar.

"Sirens," Captain Bantu exclaimed. "Probably the most haunting, twisted evolutionary mishap to come out of the Dead Time. Don't know what they started out as. Don't know if it was century of mutation, the byproduct of interspecies mating. Who knows? There's plenty of stories on the sea. I don't believe most of them. But I know what I've seen and what I've seen is about as terrifying as anything I've ever encountered in my decades upon the Great Northern Sea."

Captain Bantu drew in another mouthful of smoke, savored it upon his pallet, then exhaled.

"What are they?" Kav asked.

"Science has yet to figure that out," Captain Bantu admitted.

"What are you talking about?" Kav continued, his voice tinged with both frustration and curiosity.

"I'm talking about a creature that lures men to their death. Their songs call men toward the water. Then they pulled them and down never to be seen again."

Captain Bantu raised his left hand above his shoulder then jerked it down to demonstrate of what he spoke.

"And you don't know what they look like?" Kav asked.

"No one's lived to say. I've only seen men sucked into the depths," Captain Bantu replied.

Kav sat in deep thought then smiled.

"Wait! You're screwing with us, aren't you?"

"Of course, I am!" Captain Bantu laughed. "Those are humpbacks you hear. Whales."

Kav balled up his napkin and tossed it across the table at Captain Bantu.

"You ass!" Kav cackled. "You had me going there."

"I think I had all of you," Captain Bantu laughed.

24

───────

"You're about to see how we make a living," Captain Bantu exclaimed.

Taylor stared out the front window of the bridge.

"Not out there," Captain Bantu exclaimed. He pointed to a display screen that sat before man named Jake. "About 9,000 feet below us."

The color display featured a series of gray football-like shapes in a sea of blue.

Jake pulled a mic from the top of his head to before his mouth.

"All hands-on deck," Jake announced over the ship's intercom. "The hunt starts in three...Two...One."

Jake pushed the button to the right of the display.

"ED fired."

Taylor looked to Captain Bantu. "ED?"

"Watch the screen," Captain Bantu replied, pointing to the display. "You'll see it in a minute or two. It's a small torpedo. ED stands for echolocation disruptor. It sends out a blast that scrambles their ability to use their echolocation."

"Echolocation?" Ravaa asked, entering the bridge, a look of excitement on her face.

"It's how they see down in the depths," Captain Bantu explained.

"Like bats. They send out a signal. It bounces back to them. What we just shot down there disrupts that and sends them scrambling to the surface."

"There it is," Taylor said pointing at the screen. An elongated orange line was descending quickly from the top of the screen.

"Watch the whales," Captain Bantu instructed Taylor and Ravaa. "Watch them on the screen."

The orange object reached the center of the screen where it was surrounded on all sides by gray football shapes that represented whales.

"Disruption in three...two...one," Jake said. He pressed a button on the console before him and the whale avatars on the screen scrambled then shot for the surface.

"Come on," Captain Bantu said, pulling Ravaa by the hand and out the door. Taylor followed. Captain Bantu led them to the walkway outside the bridge. The deck before and below them was a flurry of activity.

"Curly!" Captain Bantu yelled. A man with a gray beard and a black and blue face and flattened nose turned around and looked upward and to his captain. "Man the harpoon?"

"What happened to that guy's face?" Taylor asked.

"Said he tripped in the engine room," Captain Bantu said. "Fell flat on his face."

Ravaa kept a small laugh from escaping by putting her hand to her mouth.

Curly ran to the bow of the ship and jumped into a ball turret gun. He donned the headset, fired up the heads-up display, and turned the gun that he sat upon to the right 90° then back to the left 180° and then back to where it was facing forward.

"Surfacing!" Jake bellowed over the ship's speakers.

"Eyes forward, Miss Ravaa," Captain Bantu instructed. "I guarantee, you've never seen anything like this."

The ocean 75 yards before the *Northern Butcher* frothed then stormed in an unbelievable geyser. A dark bluish-black monolith exploded upward and towards the sky. Its blockhead parted to reveal a set of monstrous peg-like teeth streaming in torn tissue and flesh. The figure continued upward, growing in size and magnitude. Flukes cut from the water like wings from some prehistoric monstrosity.

"Mother of God," Ravaa cried in a mixture of fear and elation.

The creature let loose a bellow that shook the ship, then contorted sideways and collapsed back into the sea in an explosion of ocean.

"A bull," Captain Bantu exclaimed. "Ninety feet at least."

Curly fired. The blast echoed across the ship and a four-foot harpoon rocketed over the water and into the side of the creature.

"Cable detached! Curly yelled over the intercom. "Float away."

A folded block of plastic the size of a truck shot into the water. The whale roared in pain and dove. The float hit the water and inflated to three times its size.

Dozens of whales breached from the depths. Some rocketing from the deep like the bull before it had and others only exposing the top of their head or back.

Curly's harpoon gun boomed again. A harpoon shot through the air and drove into the flesh of another bull, this one, only 30 yards off the starboard side of the ship

"Cable detached," Curly's voice cried once more over the PA. "Float away."

The water before the *Northern Butcher* was a storm of confusion and violence. Two harpooned bulls flailed about in sheer determination to dive but unable to because of the monstrous buoys attached to them. Leviathans breached in confusion. Water turned. Waves grew. The ship rose and fell upon the melee. The air was a fog of seawater and blood and groans and cries.

The harpoon gun boomed once more.

"God dammit," Curly howled at his miss.

"That's it," Captain Bantu sighed.

"What?" Ravaa asked.

"There's a narrow window to all this," Captain Bantu explained, gesturing to the sea before him. "Once they hit the surface, we've got a short amount of time before they realize they're being hunted.

Taking two whales in that time is good. Three is uncommon and four is a damn miracle."

"You are definitely right," Ravaa exclaimed, her voice singing in excitement. "I've never seen anything like that."

"Then I take it you've never harpooned a shark either."

"No."

"Then today is a day of many firsts."

25

"Ravaa, this is Gus," Captain Bantu offered.

Ravaa shook hands with the man. He was tall and lean and had a mess of thick blonde hair atop his head and wore dark glasses that were singed tightly to his face by a black cord.

"We met briefly when you came on board," Gus reminded.

Ravaa didn't remember this but smiled, nonetheless.

"Gus, I want you to take Miss Ravaa out on the retrieval have her shoot us some steaks," Captain Bantu instructed.

Gus nodded and said, "Sounds like a plan."

Gus led Ravaa down through the bowels of the ship and to the stern ramp. The area was bustling with men prepping two retrieval boats.

"We're in this one," Gus said, pointing to one of the two 35-foot Pangas.

Ravaa walked to the boat. Although long, it was fairly narrow. It carried two large outboard motors and above these was a large metal frame that held several pulleys and cables. There were three men prepping the boat and Gus quickly introduce them to Ravaa.

"Let's put you up front," Gus said, pointing to the bow.

Ravaa nodded and climbed aboard. She looked around the boat then asked, "Where's the lifejackets?"

The trio of men laughed.

Ravaa looked to Gus.

"We don't wear them," Gus exclaimed. "You wouldn't last two minutes if you fell in the water."

"The whales?" Ravaa asked.

"No," Gus replied. "The sharks."

Gus and the trio of sailors entered the boat. The ramp dropped and Gus piloted the craft into the sea. He circled around the *Northern Butcher* and to the first whale taken.

The beast was still fighting the float and the result of such formed waves four and five feet high.

"Excuse me miss," the sailor named Bolin said to Ravaa.

The man maneuvered to in front of Ravaa shouldered a rocket rifle. Gus maneuvered the boat to the side of the leviathan. The beast thrashed about fought to dive. Bolin took aim and fired. The rocket pierced the creature's flat head and disappeared. A slight pop echoed across the water and the whale fell still. Ravaa looked back to Gus.

"Bolt gun," Gus said. "Similar to what they use on cattle."

Ravaa nodded.

Gus piloted the boat to the rear of the whale then gave the wheel to a sailor named Merritt. Gus walked forward, took a harpoon gun from the vertical rack, and gestured for Ravaa to stand. She did and for the first time saw the water below her teeming with sharks. Grayish silver shapes darted beneath the boat in every direction. She looked to the whale carcass and saw them ripping into the downed leviathan's flesh.

"Yep," Gus said. "That's why we've got to get him on board. They'll eat him to the bone if we leave him here much longer."

Gus pointed to the whale's tail fluke floating just below the surface of the water.

"Shoot him right there."

Ravaa shouldered the harpoon gun and fired. The dart shot through the air, pierced the water, and drove into the whale's tail. Gus took the cable spool from Ravaa's rifle and hooked it onto a cable that ran over the rear metal frame above the engine. He took the rifle from Ravaa, affixed another metal cable spool, loaded it with another harpoon, and handed it back to the woman before him.

"Hit the other fluke," Gus instructed.

Ravaa did as she was told, and Gus once again hook the cable to the boats rigging. He reloaded the harpoon gun with another spool of cable, handed it back to Ravaa, and pointed to the frenzy of sharks ripping apart the whale before him.

"We want a small one. Four to five feet in length," Gus instructed. "Good eating size."

Ravaa looked to the massive writhing grayish silver objects. They fought their way to the leviathan's open wound and pulled huge chunks of flesh into their jaws. The melee was a storm of dagger sharp teeth, gray sandpaper hides, and cold black eyes. The water was slicked in blood and oil.

"What are they?" Ravaa asked, shouldering her rifle.

"Whites. Great whites," Gus replied.

Ravaa took aim at a smaller shark on the fringe of the school. Its body was scarred and half its dorsal fin missing. Ravaa fired. The bolt hit just in front of the sharks second dorsal fin and the beast twisted and spun madly. Gus took the rifle, attached the cable to the rigging, and took his place behind the wheel.

"Hang on!" Gus cried.

26

The whale was dragged up the stern ramp and the retriever boat hoisted into its hold.

Taylor, Donovan, Ruby, and Kav stood watching the process unfold. Ravaa and Gus joined them.

"That is one hell of a catch!" Kav exclaimed.

"Yep," Gus agreed with Kav's take on the leviathan. "And got another one coming up here shortly."

"Another shark?" Kav joked.

Ravaa rolled her eyes at the comment.

"Ha!" Gus said. "Just one shark."

Taylor walked to the whale. He, like the rest of his team, had never seen one out of the water and all were amazed at what they saw. The beast was nearly black in color and was covered in long deep scars and puncture marks. His lower jaw was riddled with barnacles and carried what Gus called whiskers that measured three to six feet in length.

"What's their purpose?" Taylor asked of Gus. "Sperm whales on earth don't have them, do they?"

Gus shook his head from side to side.

"Not on Earth. No," Gus said. "Don't know what if anything

they're for. A mutation of some sort. Might help them with feeding. Only the males have them."

Gus put the whale's length at 96 feet and carrying a weight of nearly 100 tons.

"How old?" Ravaa asked.

Gus walked to the jaws and examined the wear on the teeth.

"Maybe 40 to 50 years old," Gus said, before turning his head toward the open sea. "That's the other boat. Thank you for your help but things in here are about to get bloody."

Taylor thanked Gus for his time and led his team back to the upper deck.

27

———————

Dinner was served on the deck under the stars. Taylor and his entire team plus Captain Bantu sat eating shark steaks, fried barnacles taken from the two whales' jaws, and grilled kebabs of leviathan, onion, jalapeño, and tomato. Wine flowed freely and the crowd told and retold of what they had witnessed that day. The plates were cleared and tables taken away and drinks poured and cigars and cigarettes lit.

Gus appeared from the darkness and before him stood a sailor with what appeared to be a cow horn. The man blew the horn and it trumpeted a God-awful sound that brought about hearty laughs and nervous cackles from those watching.

"Now that we have your attention," Gus said. "Miss Ravaa, would you please stand."

Ravaa looked to her friends for explanation, but they offered none, only the encouragement to rise. Ravaa stood and Gus walked toward her.

"I am proud to present to you a token of appreciation to our newest whaler."

Gus brought his hands from behind his back to reveal a necklace of shark teeth. The center tooth was taken from a leviathan and measured some five inches in length.

Ravaa beamed and turned her back to allow Gus to tie the leather cord around her neck. She ran her fingers over the teeth then turned to her team and to cheers of excitement and catcalls.

"Thank you," Ravaa said in response. She turned to Gus. "And thank you."

"That's the smallest whale tooth we could find on your leviathan. Anything much larger and I do believe you'd develop permanent neck damage wearing it."

Taylor asked for Gus and his companion to join the group but Gus excused himself saying there was still work to be done on the whales down below.

Ravaa allowed everyone a close inspection of her necklace then returned to her seat.

The group continued drinking, smoking, and celebrating until Captain Bantu excused himself for the evening. This started a chain reaction in which Arnie said he should return to the monitoring of his equipment, Donavan and Ruby saying they'd take the first night's watch, and Kav saying he was heading below to catch some sleep before taking the second watch. Taylor and Ravaa said good night to all and each agreed they were far from a point where they were ready to turn in.

Ravaa was still swimming in adrenaline from her day of new experiences and Taylor was enjoying his cigar and tequila. Ravaa killed her cigarillo in the ashtray next to her. Taylor saw this and pulled two fresh cigars from his shirt pocket. He gestured to Ravaa with tequila, and she nodded in the affirmative. Taylor cut the cigars and they both lit up. Ravaa topped off each of their tequilas then raised her glass.

"To the *Northern Butcher's* newest whaler," Taylor offered.

Ravaa let loose a slight chuckle then toasted and the two drank.

Taylor stared upward at the stars and allowed his thoughts to drift. The assignment thus far had been uneventful in terms of encountering the target, but he suspected that this would soon change now that they had entered into prime whaling territory. He took a puff on his cigar then blew some smoke rings towards the heavens then dropped his head and caught Ravaa's eyes.

"You still haven't figured it out yet, have you?" Ravaa pondered.

Taylor's eyebrows raised in question.

"What?" he asked.

"I've seen the way you look at me."

Taylor started to protest.

Ravaa continued, "You look at me like you know me, but you can't quite place me. I'll make it easy for you. We never met before you hired me."

Taylor was taken aback. The woman before him looked familiar but he had yet to be able to place why she looked so. The fact that she just admitted that she'd never met him perplexed him even more so.

Ravaa took a heavy drink of her tequila.

"Okay," she said. "I'll spare you the theatrics. You knew my father."

Taylor searched his memory but found no answers.

"Gray," Ravaa finally admitted. "My father was Gray."

Taylor's mind flooded back a decade to the Ranger that had helped him. The man who insured that he had rescued Dej and helped him seek revenge on the man who had taken her and brutally murdered his parents. It was because of Gray that Taylor now worked for Shun. And it was because Taylor worked for Shun that he had hired Ravaa.

Taylor searched for the right words to say.

"Gray. He never mentioned..."

"I doubt he would have," Ravaa began anew. "He didn't know about me until I was 14. And he made it very clear I was a mistake from his past that he wanted nothing to do with."

"I'm..."

"Don't be," Ravaa interrupted. "I made my peace with it."

Taylor felt that Ravaa hadn't made her piece with such knowledge. She seemed distance and her earlier comment was contrived. He was made uncomfortable by this. He tried to lighten the mood.

"You do look like him," Taylor finally said. "The eyes especially."

Ravaa gave a slight smile.

"They're the same blue," Taylor continued.

"I got his blood, not his blessing in life. Or his name."

"You shoot as well as he did. Better even."

"I guess there is something to be said for genetics."

Ravaa paused to enjoy her cigar. She killed her tequila then poured another. Taylor killed his and lifted his glass. Ravaa topped them off then returned to her seat.

"Okay. I told you my story," Ravaa started fresh. "You tell me his final one. How did he die? I've heard the rumors. Now, I'd like to hear it from the only other person alive to witness it. If I got that part right that is."

Taylor thought for a moment.

"Yes. That's true. I'm the only one left alive to have seen it. Everyone else there at the time is dead."

Taylor took a drink.

"Your father..." Taylor paused unsure if that's how she wanted the late Ranger to be referred to. He began anew. "Gray died saving my life. And the lives of many young women."

Taylor told of how he met Gray through Shun and how Shun had assigned Gray to help him track down the Descendants that had kidnapped his girlfriend and many other women.

"The group was led by an outcast that believed himself a throwback to some ancient Martian civilization," Taylor continued. "He called himself the New God of Mars. He killed families up and down the frontier. Took only women. And then when he had them in his group..."

The look on Ravaa's face said she understood what happened next.

Taylor skipped to the end of the story.

"Gray and I found them. We were both injured. Badly. The New God ran a spear through Gray's body. Gray smiled, pulled himself along the shaft towards his attacker, and decapitated him."

"Cut his head off! How..."

"With these."

Taylor twisted his wrists. Eight-inch-long blade shot forward from the gauntlets he wore.

Ravaa's eyes grew in disbelief. She'd never seen such a weapon before.

Taylor twisted his wrists and the blades retracted.

"The gauntlets and the armor I'm wearing were his..."

"I'm sure he wanted you to have them," Ravaa admitted.

"I feel they should belong to you."

"Gray gave me everything he ever wanted me to have. His weapons and armor were never part of the package."

28

Ravaa's dreams were painted in a crash of adrenaline, too much white wine, and an overabundance of Red Crowe tequila. The visions unfolded in single pictures as if her subconscious was flipping through photo album on her comm.

The first picture presented to Ravaa was of her mother. The woman was young and beautiful and even standing in the shambles of a one room apartment in a favela she was smiling and happy. The next picture showed the same woman ravaged by illness. Ravaa's mother was gaunt, her skin thin as paper, and glistening and fevered in sweat. Her eyes were dead, void of any color or reflection, and seemed to focus on some unseen point in the far beyond.

The next picture showed Ravaa herself as a child of only 12 years old. She was huddled in a cardboard box that served as her home in a makeshift dump at the edge of the favela. It was pouring rain and Ravaa sat inside her shelter with knees held against her chest for warmth. She was streaked in filth. Her clothes were tattered and torn, and her long blonde hair matted and knotted.

This picture of homelessness twisted into a near portrait of her biological father. Gray sat in the back recesses of some dark establishment. He was dressed in the body armor and wearing the wrist gauntlets now worn by Taylor. The man that was her father held an assault rifle across his lap and the look in his eyes was one of fury and hate.

Ravaa's dream next took her to a picture of battle. She stood knife in hand over the dead body of a Descendent. His throat was split to the bone, his blood slicked hands told of his fight to stave the wound, and Ravaa's eyes showed her satisfaction at having taken his life.

These still photos gave way to a true vision of movement. Ravaa saw herself suspended in gin clear water. She hovered in space. Her striking blue eyes looked forward in awe and wonder.

Ravaa awoke.

She went to the small bathroom in her cabin. She rinsed her sweaty face with handfuls of water and dried it with a towel and returned to bed and to sleep this time without the interruption of dreams.

29

"What is it?" Taylor asked Arnie as he entered the bridge.

Captain Bantu followed Taylor and his demeanor suggested he'd like to know the same thing.

"It's well...I don't know," Arnie exclaimed, his eyes glued to the array of monitors before him.

"You called me up here for that!" Taylor barked.

"No...I mean..."

"Spit it out!" Taylor commanded.

Arnie continued staring at the screen. He wiped his sweaty brow with the palm of his hand.

"Okay...I found nothing..." Arnie confessed.

"Nothing what?" Taylor asked. "What does that mean?"

"It means the advance program I'm running told me three minutes ago that a spot a half mile off our starboard is nothing."

"What?" Captain Bantu questioned.

"Okay," Arnie groaned with a heavy sigh. "So, the system basically said there is nothing within a five-mile radius of us except for this spot a half mile out that registers as nothing."

"Nothing what?" Taylor asked. "Quit speaking in code."

"That's just it," Arnie tried to explain. "There's nothing at that point. Nothing like anything surrounding it. It doesn't register as a ship, water, as a rogue wave, a whale, or debris. It's nothing."

"It can't be nothing. It has to be something. What's your best guess?" Taylor asked.

"My best guess is that it's...something."

"Where is it now?" Taylor groaned.

Arnie pointed to the screen.

Taylor cut him short.

"In the real world?!" Taylor exclaimed. "Point to it in the real world!"

Arnie stood and pointed out the window.

"Eight hundred meters there."

Taylor walked to the open door.

An alarm sounded from one of Arnie's many electronic devices. The lights in the bridge blinked.

"What was..."

Arnie cut short Taylor's question.

"The nothing...something just hit us with an EMP."

"I thought you said..."

Arnie cut short Taylor once more.

"It, the EMP, didn't work. My system did. We just had a slight hick up."

Taylor turned to Captain Bantu, "Steer us to straight away from that point," Taylor commanded. "Open it up to full speed."

"Kantar wants you to catch whoever..." Captain Bantu began.

"My first job is to keep you and your crew alive, and I have no idea what were up against yet," Taylor explained in a rushed voice before turning to Arnie. "I want my crew at the upper stern deck. Fully armed."

30

———————

"What do you mean it didn't work?" Katanga furiously questioned.

Wang Lie kept his eyes glued to the monitors before him. He could feel Katanga staring into the back of his head from his place behind him on the bridge.

"Checking," Wang Lie stuttered.

"Was the pulse sent?" Katanga angrily questioned.

"Yes. The pulse was sent. It just didn't..."

"Didn't what?"

"Didn't work."

"He's changed course," a man named Mal seated next to Wang announced.

"Changed course?"

"He's steering away from us, sir," Mal clarified.

Katanga slammed his balled fists onto the display before him and exploded from his chair.

"They know we're here!" Katanga bellowed. "They have our position."

"Sir, there is no way..."

Katanga cut Wang Lie short.

"Defer power from stealth."

Wang Lie spun around in his chair.

"Sir?"

"Kill it!" Katanga ordered. "Divert all power to the engines. I want full speed ahead. Now!"

Wang Lie quickly turned around to face his monitor and did as instructed.

The ship lurched forward. Katanga steadied himself.

"Jam their communications," Katanga commanded Wang Lie.

Wang Lie furiously worked the flat screen before him. Sweat beaded on his forehead. His fingers shook nervously.

"It's not working," Wang Lie finally admitted.

"Who are these guys?" Mal asked.

Katanga fumed. His face tightened in rage.

"Take out every dish and antenna on that ship!"

31

K av, Donovan, Ruby, and Ravaa raced to Taylor's position upon the top stern deck of the *Northern Butcher*. The group quickly dropped gun and ammo cases at their feet and opened them and loaded their vests and belts with extra ammunition and grenades.

"Half a mile behind us," Taylor said pointing at what appeared to be just open ocean.

"Found it," Ravaa exclaimed from behind a pair of binoculars. She stared at what looked like a mirage upon the water, a boil of heat shimmering on the near horizon. The disturbance suddenly vanished. In its place appeared a black ship furiously cutting the ocean before it.

"Arnie, don't make me ask," Taylor said into the radio microphone clipped to his left shoulder.

There was no answer.

"Today, Arnie!"

The team's radio screeched in unison. Everyone rushed to turn them down.

"Sorry," Arnie began. "Having some issues up here."

"What else is new?" Kav asked into the radio.

"What?" Arnie asked.

"Cut the shit, Kav," Taylor instructed, before returning to his radio and to Arnie. "What are we up against?"

"It's the...this doesn't make sense," Arnie said.

"Today!" Taylor bellowed.

"The *Varro*. Independence Class Martian Navy. Sunk some 15 years ago. Three hundred feet in length."

"Sunk 15 years ago?" Ravaa questioned.

"Told you, doesn't make sense," Arnie shot back.

"Continue," Taylor commanded.

"Four 50 caliber guns. Two forward. Two aft. Wait..."

"Wait. What?" Taylor rebuked.

"She's trying to jam our communications."

"She can't, can she?" Ravaa asked.

"No," Arnie replied.

A distant clap of thunder sounded.

"Incoming!" Kav shouted.

A silver dart rocketed through the air and toward the *Northern Butcher*. All but Taylor ducked as the object zoomed toward them. The rocket slammed into the upper bridge. The ship lurched forward as flames tore across the upper structure of the ship. The fire alarm was sounded and crewmen ran from every direction to fight the blaze.

"Ravaa, distance?" Taylor questioned before commanding, "Kav, prep a rocket."

Ravaa stood and raised the binoculars to her face. Kav took one of the RK 17 Shoulder-Launched Multipurpose Assault Weapons from the case and stood.

"Four hundred meters," Ravaa exclaimed. "Coming in fast. Three ninety-five."

Kav locked the rocket's heads up display sight on the ship.

"Heat signature locked. Fire in the hole," he cried. He pulled the trigger and the 15-pound rocket ripped over the ocean and towards the oncoming black ship. Flares and streaks of light shot outward from the vessel.

"Countermeasures," Ravaa said.

"Son of a bitch," Taylor said.

The team watched as the rocket spun through the cloud of lights, plunged into the ocean a fair distance from the ship, and exploded.

"Load another Kav," Taylor ordered. "Donovan, load a slug."

The two men nodded and quickly did as instructed. They took their positions and anxiously awaited further orders.

"Ravaa," Taylor said.

"Three hundred eighty," Ravaa answered.

"When you're ready, Kav," Taylor said. "Donovan four seconds after. Right down their throat."

"Heat signature locked...Fire in the hole!"

The rocket screamed forward. Donovan counted his time down then fired.

32

"Countermeasures launched," Wang Lie announced.

The bridge watched as the view before them became a kaleidoscope of lights followed by a distant explosion. "The second shot's a..."

Wang Lie's warning was cut short by a sudden impact that sent all on the bridge hurling backwards. Katanga slammed to the rear wall and collapsed to the floor.

"Damage?" Katanga cried out as he stood.

Wang Lie and Mal fought their way back to their duty stations.

"Punched a hole through the bow. Above the waterline. Probably just a slug."

"Tit for tat," Katanga announced. "Send a slug right up their ass."

"Sir..." Wang Lie began.

"Up the stern ramp and through the ship..."

"Sir..." Wang Lie pleaded.

"Then ram them," Katanga continued. "We'll reach them before they sink. We'll find Taylor before he drowns."

"But sir, I can't guarantee..."

Katanga drew the pistol from his holster and pointed it at Wang Lie's head.

"Sir me one more time and I'll blow your face all over that console."

Wang Lie swallowed and nodded ever so slightly.

"Now Mr. Wang," Katanga continued. "Fire when ready."

Wang Lie locked the forward cannon on target and fired. All watched as the rocket tore above the open water and ripped through the *Northern Butcher.* The whaling ship shot upward then slammed forward. Orange flames bellowed from the bow in a storm of steel and diesel. Black smoke rose and the water churned.

"Right through them," Wang Lie reported.

Katanga burst into laughter. He swiped the screen before him and a hologram of Taylor appeared above the screen.

"Prepare to board," Katanga announced over the ships communication system. "Capture this man. Taylor. Kill everyone else."

33

———

"Incoming!" Kav warned.

"Holy shit!" Donovan cried.

The group watched as a blur of metal flew across the sea and up the stern ramp below them. The ship dropped and buckled, knocking all to the deck. An explosion at the bow shook the ship and the percussion wave blew the team back and against the railing.

Taylor and the rest of the crew scrambled to their feet.

"Arnie, come in," Taylor calmly commanded into his radio. "Status update."

The radio cackled in static.

"Arnie, come in," Taylor tried again.

There was no response.

Ruby stepped forward and looked to her team leader. Taylor nodded and Ruby ran toward the bridge.

"Distance 100 meters," Ravaa called from behind her binoculars. "Wait...there's a second ship behind her..."

"Son of a bitch's gonna ram us," Kav declared of the black warship tearing across the sea and toward them.

"Again, there's a second ship behind them," Ravaa exclaimed. "The *Red Wind*."

Ravaa's declaration was ignored.

A cacophony of distant thuds echoed across the water. This was followed by sharp whistles then by the sounds of metal clanking across the ship. A grenade landed in front of Taylor. He kicked it forward and it spiraled downward and exploded upon the surface of the water.

The team grabbed Viper rifles and extra ammo and rushed along the deck towards the center of the ship. Another flash grenade exploded some 15 feet before them. The blast threw the entire team to the deck. Taylor fought back up to a standing position to see Ruby running down the stairs towards him. Flames danced and heavy black smoke billowed behind her

"Gone!" Ruby shouted over the sound of burning wreckage and crew members fighting flames. "Bridge. Everything forward of it's gone. Leveled. Arnie and Bantu never knew what hit 'em."

"Smoke!" Donovan yelled.

Taylor spun around to see a trio of hand-sized canisters rocketing through the air towards them. The grenades dropped to the deck blew apart in a tornado of thick black smoke. Three more canisters dropped to the deck, exploded, and choked the ship in an ink black cloud.

"Go thermal!" Taylor coughed to his team.

He worked the contact lens controller at his wrist and the world before him turned into a patchwork of heat signatures. He pulled the shemagh at his neck up over his mouth and nose and made his way to the railing. The darkness before him became a lightning storm of blurred colors and 50 caliber fire that stitched up the starboard side of the boat.

The gunfire ceased and the heat signature of the black warship appeared.

"Hang on!" Taylor screamed.

The *Varro* plowed into the *Northern Butcher* at its stern. The attack ship plowed forward, grinding metal until it came to rest parallel to the whaleship. A horde of human heat signatures rushed forward and onto the *Northern Butcher*. Taylor dropped into a crouch, shouldered his Viper, and began picking targets.

The deck was a frenzy of violence and the sounds of close quarters battle. Gunfire rioted. Machetes and knives came together in metallic screams. Men yelled in surprise and in pain.

The smoke slowly dissipated to reveal a stage of combat. Men and women were fighting hand-to-hand, bullets pierced flesh, and machetes sliced muscle. Bone was broken or crushed. Stun grenades flashed. Percussion waves tore across the deck.

34

---

avaa put two holes center mass into the first signature to jump from the *Varrow* and onto the *Northern Butcher*. The figure slammed backward and over the railing. A horde of glowing white figures pushed through the smoke like some spectral dream toward her. Ravaa held aim and took the next marauder down with two shots to the chest. A sudden flash of light blinded her. Something heavy kicked her in the chest. She fell backward at the impact, rolled over, and started to stand. She put her left hand on her rifle. A man's boot came down heavy on her hand. She grunted in pain, pulled her pistol, pushed it into the man's ankle before her, and fired. Fabric, blood, bone, and muscle showered forth. The man fell over and on top of Ravaa. The two rolled over and over in a race for dominance.

Ravaa jammed her pistol into the man's shoulder and fired twice. The man howled in agony. He released his grip on Ravaa. She lunged forward and fired twice more into the man's abdomen. The man yelped in pain then began laughing hysterically. He pulled a grenade from his vest and tossed it just before him. Ravaa saw it. It was a percussion grenade. She turned and ran then felt the blast before she heard it. The force knocked her forward and onto the railing. The breath was knocked out of her. Something slammed into her back. She spun around just in time to catch a bullet in the chest. The impact knocked her over the railing and somersaulting downward and into the Great Northern Sea.

35

———————

Katanga was pleasantly surprised at the ease with which his crew was taking over the *Northern Butcher*. He had feared, given their possessing shoulder launched rockets, that they would be a more formidable enemy. This proved not to be the case.

Katanga followed the three gunmen before him onto the deck of the huge whaling ship. The black smoke from the grenades was thinning and the sight before him was one of crewmen being shot, beaten, or stabbed to death by his men. A woman in full combat gear rushed forward. She was streaked in filth and blood and her eyes flashed in frenzied bloodlust. She raised the pistol in her hand and fired and kept firing as she ran forward.

Katanga's men opened fire. Bullet after bullet from their fully automatic carbines slammed into the bloodied warrior. She spasmed at each impact, jerked backward as if being pulled by a marionette's strings, then collapsed upon the deck. Katanga stepped to before his men and took the fallen woman by the hair upon the back of her head. He lifted her face from the deck. She glared at him. Katanga smiled and raised the machete in his free hand. The woman spat out a wad of bloody phlegm in one last defiant act.

A male screamed across the deck.

"No!"

Katanga looked up to see a young man in combat gear running toward him. Katanga's smile widened at the man's concern. He raised the machete slightly higher then brought it down and through the woman's neck. Katanga stood and laughed at the sight the woman's severed head rolling on the deck. He pointed his blood-soaked machete at the soldier running toward him. Katanga's men shot the man's kneecaps out from under him. He crumbled to the deck in excruciating pain. Katanga approached the man and grabbed him by the short hair atop his head.

"Honor her," Katanga instructed the man. "Say her name."

The man grimaced in pain.

Katanga raised the man's head by the chin with his machete.

"What is her name?"

The man spat, "Her name *was* Ruby. I'm Donovan. And I swear to God..."

Katanga nodded and one of his men put a pistol to the back of Donovan's head and blew his brains onto the deck.

36

———

Ravaa slammed into the ocean, the impact against her back knocking the wind from her body. She fought the churning waves and coughed and flailed about in an effort to right herself. She sank beneath the surface. She holstered her pistol and kicked upward for all her life. She broke the surface and entered into a storm of gunfire. Bullets rained down on her. She took a deep breath and dove. She swam downward as fast as she could, letting the weight of her body armor and weaponry assist in the endeavor.

The water was thick with debris. Whale oil and diesel fuel swirled in thin ribbons. Clouds of blood slowly rained downwards. Bullets spent of all their energy showered from above.

Ravaa fought through and around this and to beneath the slowly sinking ship. She made her way to the air tanks her team had installed along the keel and took the regulator in her mouth, taking in a lungful of air. She fought to calm herself and plan her next move. A blur of motion caught Ravaa's eye. She looked downward to see dark shapes circling upward from the depths. They rose in ever tightening circles then rocketed straight upward in attack. The sharks took the dead or dying in their jaws. They ripped limbs from bodies and shook muscle from bone. The water turned crimson red.

Kav swam down through the intermittent clouds of blood and toward the air tanks. Ravaa held out one of the regulators for him. He quickly took it in his mouth and engulfed a huge lungful of air.

He suddenly shot up and into the steel keel of the ship. His body from the waist down was in the jaws of a monstrous great white shark. Kav flailed about. The regulator was ripped from his mouth. He pounded his fists into the shark. The monstrous predator violently shook Kav until his body halved.

The shark grabbed the upper half of Kav in its jaws and dove downward and out of sight. Ravaa pulled her pistol and scanned the water around her. A small shark of about four feet rocketed toward her. Ravaa raised her pistol. The predator plowed forward. It opened its jaws. Ravaa jerked to the side of the fish and shoved her pistol point blank into the side of the shark's head just behind his eye and fired. The 10 mm round pushed through the shark's sandpaper hide and out the other side in a thick cloud of blood.

37

Taylor fired the last bullet from his Viper near point-blank into the neck of the man before him. The marauder grabbed his throat and toppled backward. Taylor spun the rifle in his hands and swung it butt end first as a club into the side of the head of the next man to come at him. The man tripped sideways and fell over. Taylor threw his rifle at the next man to come at him and hit him square in the face. He drew his pistol. A silver web sailed toward him.

The net engulfed Taylor and an electric current shot through his body. He spasmed in pain and collapsed to his knees. He snapped his wrists releasing the eight-inch blades from their gauntlets and cut through the electrified net containing him. He bolted upright and to his feet. More than 10 men stood before him including the man he recognized as Katanga. The pirate leader stood, holding a blood-soaked machete at his side. Taylor shot back his arms and the blades extended from them out wide and challenged, "Let's go!"

Katanga pointed at Taylor with his machete and ordered his men, "Take him!"

Katanga's men raced forward. They circled Taylor and took to him with clubs, rifle butts, and Taser pistols. They converged on Taylor and did all they could to beat him to the ground. Taylor fired his pistol twice into the mob. Someone wrestled the pistol from his hand. Taylor continued fighting with fists and kicks and swipes of blades but, in the end, fell to the overwhelming odds.

38

———————

Ravaa watched the sharks while formulating her plans of attack. She started with what she knew as fact.

Arnie and Captain Bantu were dead.

She saw Ruby and Donovan executed.

Kav had just been consumed by a shark.

When she last saw Taylor, he was holding his own against the onslaught.

The *Northern Butcher* was slowly sinking as was the ship that attacked them.

A constant yet distant whirl cut through the water. The noise grew louder. Ravaa circled around to ensure the area was more or less shark free, took a deep breath of air, and swam along the bottom of the ship and to the surface. She came up behind some floating debris to see the *Red Wind* speeding towards her. The ship came up alongside the partially submerged *Varro*. She watched as men left the *Northern Butcher* and made their way upon the *Red Wind*. She saw a group carrying Taylor. He was either dead or unconscious although she doubted the former given that they were carrying him and had killed everyone else.

Or, in her case, tried.

Ravaa studied the rear of the ship. A ladder came halfway down the stern of the ship but stood some 15 feet above the water's surface. She took a deep breath and dove for the air tanks beneath that she'd just left. She reached them, took several puffs of air, then swam beneath the ship to the stern ramp.

She swam in and surfaced in an air pocket. The interior hold was in tatters. The missile that the *Varro* had shot through the whaler had left it a twisted heap of metal and mess of melted plastic. The two recovery ships were smashed almost beyond recognition.

Ravaa swam about the cratered boats until she found one of the harpoon guns. She loaded it, checked the spool and line, then dove beneath the oil slicked water. She swam through streams of blood and whale oil and shredded clothing and debris back to the submerged air tanks. She paused to replenish her air then heard the prop churn of the *Red Wind* growing in strength.

She pushed off the bottom of the whaleship and swam as fast as she could to the massive ship. She surfaced behind it just as the prop was engaged. The chop pushed her backward. She quickly raised the gun and fired at the bottom rung of the ladder. The harpoon shot between two bottom rungs, bounced off the hull, and fell behind the ladder. The momentum of the ship pulled the line tight and Ravaa quickly pulled herself to the boat and climbed the cable and onto the ladder. She held tight to the structure watching what was left of the two ships gently toss in the ship's wake.

"What the hell do I do now?" she exhaustively asked herself.

Ravaa didn't pause to think of an answer to her question. Instead, she attached herself to the ladder with a carabiner from her vest. She pulled the pistol from her leg holster, reloaded it with a magazine from her vest, then made note of how much ammo she had left. She reloaded the harpoon gun and slung it over her shoulder then pulled the comm from her vest pocket to find it dead.

"Waterproof my ass," she complained.

She put the comm back in her pocket the tested her radio. It too was dead. She pulled it from her vest and tossed it into the chop below. She watched it disappear beneath the white prop foam then looked past the ship's wake to watch the two battle damaged ships slip deeper and deeper into the drink.

39

———————

Taylor awoke.

He found himself sprawled upon the floor of a small room the walls, ceiling, and ground of which were worn metal. There was no furniture or plumbing to speak of. He was in his cell of some sort. He rolled over and put his ear to the cold metal floor. He could feel a slight vibration against his face and could barely make out the faint grinding of metal and the sound of engines turning.

He was on a ship.

One that was moving quickly.

He sat up.

The pain in his head and aches in his body rushed downward and flooded his gut. He felt he might be sick. The feeling passed after a moment. He ran his hands over his face to assess the damage inflicted by the men that had beaten him into unconsciousness. His lower jaw was bruised and swollen. He had several small cuts on his cheeks and his nose was fractured. He moved to the back of his head to find two small knots and a few more cuts.

He stood.

He was absent his body armor and wrist gauntlets and his shirt was ripped in several places. He searched both his shirt and pants pockets to find them empty.

There was a sudden sound of metal grinding. The door opened. Two large men entered. They were followed by Katanga. The pirate leader looked Taylor over and sneered in disgust.

"Someone wants to see you," Katanga spat.

40

———

Darkness fell upon the Great Northern Sea.

Ravaa watched as the setting sun bathed the wake of the *Red Wind* and the ocean beyond it in hues of crimson and apricot. These colors quickly faded into gray then gave way to darkness. Ravaa unhooked her carabiner and quickly sulked up the ladder. She peered over the bulwark to find the deck deserted. She quickly made her way over the guard railing and into a flat crouch next to the outer wall of some sort of cabin or structure. She pulled her pistol and move stealthily against the wall and towards its edge. She paused at the end and looked around the corner. She saw no one. She pulled her head back.

The air was suddenly filled with the sounds of men. Ravaa heard coughing, complaints, and the clearing of throats. She slinked through the darkness and along the wall to an overlook. Below her on the center deck stood gathered a group of nearly 20 men.

41

The two men secured Taylor's wrists before him with plastic ties and led him out of the makeshift cell. The pirates and their prisoner followed Katanga down a narrow hallway sweating in peeled paint and rust and up several flights of stairs. They exited onto a deck bathed in artificial light populated by 15 to 20 men. Taylor saw that some of these carried fresh injuries earned when they boarded the *Northern Butcher*. Taylor's two escorts pushed him to the deck and upon his knees.

A hulking figure dressed in black clothing and black body armor strode to the front of the assembly. The dark figure's legs and right arm were subject to an exoskeleton and most of his face stood covered in a mask of heavy plastic and wires. What skin the man did have visible was thin and scarred.

"Taylor," the man said, his voice strained and muffled behind his mask.

Taylor stared straight ahead ignoring the calling of his name.

The man unhooked the left side of his mask with his right hand to reveal a jawline of raw muscle and absent of lips.

Taylor studied the man in shock and disgust then voiced his astonished revelation.

"Powell! But you're..."

"Dead? No. I'm very much alive. And almost to the point of controlling the Great Northern Sea."

Hundreds of images flashed through Taylor's head. He lay witness to he and Powell fighting together during their time in the Corps, their days spent on R&R, and, finally, of him having to leave his friend to die.

"The bombing run..." Taylor finally exclaimed in a search for understanding.

Powell's disfigured face twisted in further disgust. He slowly affixed the mask back to his face then gasped in breath. He stepped forward and toward his old friend.

"Fire rained down through the favelas. Burned through the bodies of those that had overtaken me. It ravaged over my skin, hollowed out my lungs and forever destroyed my nerves."

Taylor's defenses took control.

"You...you told me to leave you," Taylor sputtered. "You ordered me to go."

"I did. And because I did, you lived."

Powell gestured to his men who in turn lifted Taylor to his feet.

"But I did far better than live," Powell explained. "I was reborn. Given a new sense of clarity. A new enlightenment. I realized what I had to do."

Taylor was thrust back and into the present and to his mission in hand. He was where he was because the man before him had killed thousands of people in cold blood, decimated property, and rounded up women and children to sell as sexual slaves. The man before Taylor wasn't Powell. The man before Taylor was twisted and evil.

"Your enlightenment, your realization from the firing bombing was to start killing everyone you encounter on the open sea?" Taylor raged. "To kidnap women and children to sell into slavery."

Taylor edged forward.

His captives jerked him back.

"My realization was that I will take what I want," Powell barked through the confines of his mask. "And what I want is..."

"No one cares!" Taylor yelled. "Especially not the children you took or..."

"Who are you to lecture me?" Powell almost screamed. "Do you not work for Shun? The man rules the planet."

"I made a deal to save the one I love..."

Powell took a step back and fought to ingest several deep breaths. He stepped forward once more and to before former comrade in arms. The men on either side of Taylor tightened their grip on his arms.

"I didn't bring you here to quarrel," Powell assured Taylor. "I brought you here to join me."

Taylor shook his head in revulsion.

"Join me," Powell repeated. "Together, we will take what we deserve..."

"You deserve to have died in that shit hole I left you in."

Powell reared back and drove his heavy leather clad glove into Taylor's gut. Taylor dropped to his knees and fought to breathe. Powell grabbed Taylor's hair and pulled his head back so he gazed upward.

"Chess tells me that Kantar wants you to bring me before him," Powell spat.

Taylor's eyes glazed in pure rage.

"Tomorrow, I will bring you before him!"

42

———————

Ravaa could just make out what the man named Powell had said. It was a lot to process. The most important pieces of information she heard was that Powell was taking Taylor before Kantar Saber tomorrow. She assumed Powell meant Kantar's compound. If that truly was the case, then she would have to slip off the ship to warn the crime boss and to hopefully gather reinforcements to rescue Taylor. All she had to do until then was stay hidden. She sunk backward and away from the railing. She slinked around the corner and to the place where she had first climbed aboard the *Red Wind.*

"Hey!" the pirate's voice was deep and peppered in surprise.

Ravaa unslung her harpoon gun

The pirate unslung his rifle.

Ravaa raised her gun and fired. The long metal shaft flew forward and through the pirate's neck. The man grabbed his throat and fell to his knees. Ravaa rushed forward and put her hand over the man's mouth to keep him from screaming. She drew the knife at her vest and sliced what remained of the pirate's neck. The man spasmed once then quickly slid into death. Ravaa sheathed her knife and pulled the spear from the man's neck. She quickly reloaded the harpoon gun and placed it at her side. She took the dead man's rifle and the water bottle from his belt. She pushed him to the bulwark then flipped him over and into the sea below. She used what liquid was in the water bottle to clean the deck of blood then threw the vessel into the sea as well. She checked the rifle to find its 30-round magazine at capacity. She slung the rifle and harpoon gun over her shoulders and climbed down the ladder and into the darkness to hide.

43

Taylor was awoken by the sound of the metal door to his cell grinding open. The two pirates from the day before entered and this time bound Taylor's wrists behind his back. The men each took an arm and led Taylor through the bowels of the ship and up to the forward deck. It was dawn.

The deck was a flurry of activity with armed men gearing up for an assault. Katanga smirked at the sight of Taylor then held stoic at the approach of Powell.

"Time to watch your employer die," Powell said.

Taylor ignored the comment.

"We'll venture in under the cover of darkness. They'll never see us coming," Powell paused a moment as if deep in thought. "Just like old times."

"We never used stealth and EMPs," Taylor reminded. "We were warriors."

"Warriors fighting for someone else. Now I fight for myself. And the spoils are mine." Powell paused once more. "Reconsider, Taylor. Join me."

"Pass."

44

Chess exited the elevator to Kantar's upper lounge. The area was dark and illuminated only by a few glowing mosquito coils in the predawn starlight. The ceiling fans wafted intermittently stirring a breeze on those sleeping below. Kantar reclined in the center of the couch, his obese shirtless frame oozing in between the massive cushions. Two topless women were draped upon him, one on each side and each with their cheeks glued in sweat to his tattooed chest. Fred the lizard slept at his feet and his six guards long since fallen victim to too much hash sat slumped in chairs their rifles held tight across their laps.

Chess ignored what disgusted him and walked to the edge of the room. He pulled back the bellowing gauze curtains and stared out at the darkness that was the Great Northern Sea. The water was ink black and dully reflected the myriad of stars above. Chess stared across this expanse looking for the *Red Wind*. He knew, of course, that its stealth would render it nearly invisible, but he thought perhaps in his arrogance that he might be able to see it. His eyes wandered closer to the shore and to the long dock and stretched out into the sea for more than 100 yards. There, three guards stood rifles in hand beneath the last lamppost watching the water.

The lights along the dock suddenly went dark. Chess looked towards the city of Aruna to find it completely dark. He turned his attention upward to see the ceiling fans slowly churning to a stop. He smiled knowing that the EMP had been unleashed and that Powell would be there soon.

He kept watch on the end of the dock. The men milled about in the starlight as if looking for something. Dawn slowly broke and brought a better view of the men into play. Two of the guards worked at the base at the furthest lamppost apparently in an attempt to get the light to return. Something caught their attention and all three ran to the end of the deck. They lowered into a crouch and aimed their rifles towards a mirage. This distortion dissipated to reveal a huge black ship. The men flew backwards as their head flowered in red mist in the muted light. The craft came alongside the dock in a group of 20 or so men disembarked. All wore body armor and were armed to the teeth. The men carried before them rifles and machetes and wore pistols and knives and spare ammunition. Chess smiled at the sight and even more so at the recognition of Katanga and Powell. Chess' smile grew even wider at the sight of Taylor with his hands tied behind him.

The group advanced forward along the deck and to the shore then toward the base of the massive room.

Chess turned to survey the room once more. All were still asleep.

The first of Powell's men slinked in from the darkness of the outer stairwell. The lizard raised its head and released a bellowing hiss. Kantar's guards jump from their chairs and unleashed hell fire. Powell's men fired in return. The open room strobed in gunfire. Orange flashes flamed in the murky light. Two of Powell's men were zipped across the chest. They spasmed then fell forward. The lizard charged towards the intruders. Two bullets tore through its head sending it spinning over and into a pool of its own blood. One of Katanga's men took a bullet to the forehead and jerked backward. Another had his vest sawed in half. He fell backward, unleashing a hail of full automatic gunfire that shredded the ceiling.

Kantar roared up from the couch tossing the two half naked

women upon him onto the floor. Both screamed in shock at the realization before them. The closest to the stairwell caught a bullet to the gut that sent her doubling over in pain. A second shot tore off the crown of her skull and sent her stumbling backward and over. Kantar bellowed in rage. He grabbed the rifles from two of his fallen men and unleashed a torrent of bullets. He charged toward the stairwell, firing into an undulating mass of pirates that twisted and danced in the storm of led projectiles cutting through body armor flesh and bone.

45

Taylor and the two men that held him by the arms were at the end of the procession. Taylor could see eight men leading the attack followed by Katanga, more pirates, then Powell. The group eased up the stairs careful of each step taken and most with their guns at the ready. The forward group reached the top and team came to a halt. The two men tightened their hold on Taylor. A long gasp of air cut the silence. Two men to either side of Taylor looked one another in question.

"Kantar's got a lizard," Taylor whispered. "A big one. Eats pirates."

Gunfire boomed down the stairwell and across the early dawn. Men screamed in the adrenaline of attack and in pain and loss. Metal shell casings rained down the stairs.

Taylor took advantage of the moment and head butted the man to his right. The man let go of Taylor and stumbled backward in a daze. Taylor kicked him in the chest and down the stairs. The second jailer grabbed Taylor around the chest in a bear hug. Taylor pushed back and slammed the man into the wall. The impact knocked the air from the man. He coughed and gasped in response. Taylor slammed his head back and into the man's nose then with his bound hands behind, his back swung them into the man's crotch. The man groaned in pain and let loose his hold on Taylor's chest. Taylor spun around and kneed the man in the crotch then kicked him in the chest and down the stairs.

Taylor leaned against the wall and quickly brought his arms under his legs, so his bound wrists were now before him. He bolted down the stairs and to the first man he'd sent there. The man began to stand. Taylor kicked him in the face. The man's nose exploded inward and into a pool of blood and cartilage. The man fell and rolled three stairs down. Taylor grabbed the man's pistol and put two shots into his forehead.

The second jailer grabbed Taylor around the legs and pulled him down. The two men rolled over and down a flight of stairs and into a tangle of limbs. Taylor shook off the fall, put the pistol to the man's ear and fired. Shards of skull and brain matter splattered the wall. Taylor wretched the man off of him and stood. He ran up the stairs and toward the assault team.

Two pirates turned about and Taylor took both out on the run with a shot to each man's head. The men fell forward and rolled down the stairs. Taylor continued running up the steps. Katanga turned and launched himself through the air and toward Taylor. Katanga slammed into Taylor's chest and the two rolled down the stairs and into the bodies of Taylor's once captives. Katanga rolled on top of Taylor, reared back and delivered a hard hook to the jaw. Taylor brought the pistol in his hand up into the side of Katanga's head. Katanga grabbed Taylor's wrist and slammed it repeatedly against the concrete steps. Taylor released the pistol then lunged up and took Katanga's nose in between his teeth and pulled the man's nose from his face. Katanga reared back and grabbed his face in shock and pain. Taylor came up and drove his fist into Katanga's throat. Katanga rolled over in pain and disbelief. Taylor stood and crushed Katanga's windpipe by bringing his booted heel down on the man's throat. Taylor took the dead man's pistol and rushed back up the stairs and into the storm of constant gunfire.

46

———————

owell was disgusted.

Beyond infuriated.

His men were being mowed down by a crime lord that was probably near comatose from smoking hash and his lackey bodyguards.

Powell watched as man after man rocketed backward in a blaze of automatic gunfire. The sounds of battle were horrifyingly loud. Gunfire tore across and down the stairwell. Men screamed. Shell casings plinked down concrete steps.

The sounds of gunfire came from a new direction.

Powell turned to see a now free Taylor charging up the stairwell. He shot two pirates and was taking aim on a third.

"Take him!" Powell bellowed to Katanga. "Alive!"

Katanga launched forward and down the stairwell and into Taylor. Powell watched as the two men grappled for the upper hand. Taylor ripped off Katanga's nose then punched the man in the throat. Powell smiled in pleasure at the sight almost enjoying the fact that his old friend was still the warrior he remembered.

Taylor killed Katanga with a stop of his heel and Powell fumed in a blind rage.

Taylor charged up the stairs. He put a round into the chest of the man to Powell's right. The man caved inward at the blast to his chest plate. A shot to the jaw by Taylor sent the man back and to the stairs.

"Enough!" Powell barked.

He pulled his pistol and fired. The bullet carved across Taylor's right thigh, and he dropped to his knees. Two men ran down the stairs, disarmed Taylor, and pulled him upright. The remaining two men above Powell tumbled backward in death.

"If you want something done," Powell huffed in disgust.

He reached down and picked up one of the fallen's rifles, checked it, then charged into the room.

Kantar tossed his empty rifles aside and reached down to grab another. Powell sent a bullet through the fat man's left bicep. Kantar spun around at the impact and grabbed his arm in pain. He growled in anger. Powell walked forward, his rifle held before him and at the ready.

"Looks painful," Powell toyed. He pointed to the couch with the barrel of his rifle. "Sit."

Kantar scowled. He made his way to the couch, pulled the dead half naked woman off of it, and sat.

Powell surveyed the room. He saw two dead women, six dead men, and one dead lizard.

"May I introduce, His Excellency, Kantar Saber, Eminence of the Great Northern Sea," Chess announced as he walked forward.

Kantar looked to Chess and the smirk upon his face. He looked to Powell then back to Chess and raged at the realization he had been betrayed. He started off the couch. Powell shot him a look. Kantar eased back into the couch.

"Chess," Powell said.

"Yes," Chess replied.

"Your services are no longer required."

Chess frowned.

Powell put a bullet through his head. The back of Chess' head blew outward and his body collapsed.

Kantar smiled then spat in the fallen man's direction

Taylor was brought into the room by the two men. Taylor looked to Kantar.

"You said to bring them before you," Taylor joked. "Here he is."

Kantar almost smiled.

The two men brought Taylor to next to Powell and before Kantar.

"Kantar Saber," Powell began anew. "I am taking control of the Great Northern Sea from you."

Kantar spat once more.

"So you think," Kantar said.

Powell caught a slight movement of Kantar's eyes.

Powell spun around.

Ravaa smiled.

Her rifle bellowed twice. Both of Powell's knees exploded backward. He collapsed to the floor.

Taylor wretched free of the two men and pushed them aside. Ravaa dropped both with a quick shot each to the head.

Taylor rushed forward and took Powell's rifle and the pistol in his holster. Powell fought to breathe through his heavy mask. Taylor took his old friend's shoulder in his hand and spun him around to face the ruler of the Great Northern Sea.

Kantar stood. He released the grip on his wounded shoulder. He walked to his dead lizard. He removed its heavy chain leash and walked in front of Powell.

"Your men killed my pet," Kantar declared. "I need another."

Kantar swung the leash around Powell's neck then drove the man's eyes into their sockets with his thumbs. Powell screamed. Kantar smiled at the sight before him then brought the man's head down on his knee. Powell fell to the floor and into unconsciousness.

Kantar walked to Taylor and held out his hand.

"Thank you."

Taylor shook the man's hand.

"Things don't always go according to plan," Kantar said. "But you delivered."

"I'm going to chalk this one up to Ravaa," Taylor said looking in his teammate's direction.

47

Taylor was greeted at his hotel in kind by a young redheaded woman of about 28 years of age. He never seen the woman before, yet she greeted him by name.

"Welcome back to Biānjìng House Mr. Taylor," the woman offered. "I took the liberty of preparing your room in anticipation of your arrival."

"Thank you," Taylor replied with a slight nod.

"I've also placed fresh dressings for your leg if need be, in your bathroom."

Taylor nodded once more then look down to the brace upon his leg.

"Still a little stiff, but I'll be fine. Thank you."

"Yes, sir. My name is Molly if you need anything else."

Taylor nodded for the third time and made his way to his apartment.

He had never seen his living quarters so clean. The apartment almost shined. There was a bouquet of fresh flowers on the coffee table and the room smelled of sandalwood. He dropped his bag at the door and walked to his desk. He took a cigar from the desktop humidor, snipped it, lit it, and took a few puffs. He opened the refrigerator next to his desk to retrieve a beer. He found a note labeled "Taylor" leaning against the bottles of Tsing Tsao. Taylor recognized the handwriting as Lou's. He took the note and opened it.

It read, "Taylor, I hate to end things this way but feel I have to. We have no future to speak of if you don't take care of yourself and your past. I love you and hope you find the will to address such. Bye, my love, Lou."

Taylor tossed the note upon his desk and retrieved a bottled beer. He opened it and drank. He took a puff on his cigar and said to himself on a cloud of smoke, "Well...shit."

48

———

"I feel like I'm waiting to see the principal," Ravaa exclaimed.

"Relax," Taylor said.

"Does that ever work?" Ravaa asked. "It's like telling someone to calm down. That never works."

"Point made," Taylor offered with a smirk.

Ravaa continued making her way around Shun's meeting room taking in the art and history of his many pieces.

"As long as you're not so nervous as to snap your wrists, we'll be fine," Taylor said pointing to the gauntlets upon her wrists.

Ravaa spun around, playfully growled, and flicked her wrists. Two eight-inch double-sided blades shot past her knuckles.

Taylor laughed.

"Did you just growl?" he asked.

Ravaa flicked her wrists and the blades retracted.

"Wait, I'm not supposed to growl?"

Taylor continued laughing.

"To each her own."

Ravaa beamed.

"Thank you again," she said, gesturing to the weapons upon her wrists. "It was very thoughtful of you. But unnecessary..."

The twin doors opened and Shun entered followed by Enos.

"Taylor," Shun said as he offered his hand in greeting. "I'm so pleased to see you up and about."

Taylor shook Shun's hand and gestured with his chin to his leg and offered, "It's not bad. It was just a scratch."

"A deep scratch," Ravaa joked.

Shun smiled and held out his hand to Ravaa.

"I am so pleased you are here and that you will be joining us."

Ravaa shook Shun's hand and smiled.

"Taylor has told me a great deal about you," Shun continued. "But as is his way, I'm afraid not everything. I'm at a loss for your last name or where you are from."

"It's just Ravaa. Ravaa of Mars."

ABOUT THE AUTHOR

Gayne C. Young is the author of *Murder Hornets*, the *Primal Force* series, *Bug Hunt*, *Sumatra*, *Teddy Roosevelt: Sasquatch Hunter*, *Vikings: The Bigfoot Saga*, and more. He is the Editor-at-Large for *Field Ethos Journal*, former Editor-in-Chief of *North American Hunter* and *North American Fisherman* - both part of *CBS Sports* -and a columnist for and feature contributor to *Outdoor Life* and *Sporting Classics* magazines. His work has appeared in magazines such as *Petersen's Hunting*, *Texas Sporting Journal*, *Sports Afield*, *Gray's Sporting Journal*, *Under Wild Skies*, *Hunter's Horn*, *Spearfishing*, and many others.

In January 2011, Gayne C. Young became the first American outdoor writer to interview Russian Prime Minister, and former Russian President, Vladimir Putin.

Visit Gayne at his Website or on Social Media.